# THE CLOCK

## A NOVEL

Christoher Gayle

Imagine Dat Studios

Shreveport, LA

Published in the United States by
Imagine Dat Studios
Shreveport, LA 71105

Publisher's Note: The Clock is a fanciful tale of adventure in time travel. The Hawthornes of the story are fictional. Many of the other characters are drawn from actual historical figures. Though the author does reference real historical figures, and actual locations and structures, some liberties with the facts have been taken to enhance the story.

The Clock / by Christopher Gayle -- 1st ed.

ISBN (paperback) 978-0-9963966-0-8
ISBN (e-book) 978-0-9963966-1-5

# CONTENTS

*Most importantly and especially, I dedicate this book to my precious wife Julie. She is my love, my solace and my refuge.*

# ACKNOWLEDGMENTS

Thank you to my children, Katye and Quincy, who have known of this story for years but who did not know that the children in this book were inspired by them. When I started writing this story, Katye and Quincy, grown now, were about the same ages as the characters Livi and Jack are in the book.

Finally, I would like to thank my dear friend and business partner Carl J. Lapeyrouse, who thought it would be a "cool idea" to tell a story about two children who time traveled by way of a grandfather clock and asked if I could write the story. It is Carl's children, Livi and Jack, for whom the children in this book are named.

# 1896

"Joshua!"

Lord Jonathan William Augustus Hollingsworth IV called out urgently. He was dying. Not dying in the sense that an 83-year-old man is nearing the end of his life. No, he was dying right now. How he knew this was unclear. He had no revelation, no sense of doom, no pain and no real physical ailment. Still, he knew that the end of his natural life was upon him and he had to move quickly. He wasn't afraid; he just had an overwhelming sense of urgency. He felt that he had only minutes left and he needed Joshua now.

"Joshua, can you hear me?" Why does it always take so long for him to respond? Surely it is an intentional effort to aggravate me.

Augustus sat in the near darkness of his manor library, illuminated only by the flickering light emanating from the fireplace that occupied the wall to his left. The fireplace, like the library itself, was massive. The firebox was large enough for a man to enter without stooping. But nothing in the entire manor was as massive as the object that now demanded his attention. The same object that had captured not only his attention, but also his imagination--indeed his life--for decades.

The grandfather clock that was to his right, across the room from the fireplace, was barely contained beneath the fifteen-foot ceiling. Its five-foot width was buttressed on either side by the mahogany-finished bookshelves that rose to just over two-thirds the clock's height. Indeed, the clock appeared to serve as the sentinel of the expansive room, guarding over the elongated central work table and the variously configured sitting arrangements of heavy chairs, settees, tables and footstools that were situated precisely upon the oak floors.

"Joshua, are you quite alive?" He is so infuriatingly slow!

On so many past occasions, Augustus had determined that the time had come to enter the clock. He had hypothesized, theorized and calculated until he felt he could do so no more. On paper it was flawless. But there was no way to test his work without literally committing his life to the endeavor. So, he always begged off and hypothesized, theorized and calculated some more. After all, it was a daunting proposition. Now, however, he could put it off no longer. If he didn't enter the clock now he would never know if his science proved right, and his life's work would be lost forever. He called yet again.

"Joshua, are you there?"

Being an impatient man and not considering that his faithful friend and one-time servant was two years his senior, Augustus called more loudly:

"Joshua, I say you must come now!"

Joshua Kingsley pulled on the heavy doors leading into the library, ceremoniously opening both sides simultaneously as was his custom. He entered the library, an imposing man of color still towering over six feet two inches despite the loss of height with aging. He wore, as was also his custom, a black morning coat that extended to his knees, situated over a matching waistcoat and trousers. His necktie was perfectly aligned despite the late hour. The chain of his pocket watch drooped lazily across his taut midriff and disappeared into the small pocket of his waistcoat. He walked with a cane, which Augustus felt was solely for theatrical effect, as Joshua had no difficulty ambulating. Joshua crossed the expansive room, pulled a facing chair close to Augustus, and sat.

"Tempus est, Joshua. It is time," stated Augustus softly.

In like manner, Joshua replied, "Are you sure, Augustus? You know the dangers."

Augustus bowed his head slightly in thought. Then with deliberation he sat up tall and looked Joshua in the eye, saying, "Time is of the essence. I have precious little left." Joshua, understanding the implication, stared back at Augustus for a moment. Then a wide smile materialized upon his face, turning his intimidating expression to one of benevolent kindness.

"Then let us go, my dear friend."

Augustus reached across and grasped both of Joshua's hands in his. Tears welled in his eyes as he struggled with his words.

"Thank you, my friend. It will be a grand adventure either way."

Joshua stood and cleared his chair from in front of Augustus. He bent over, disregarding his cane, and grasped Augustus under his arms. Augustus in turn reached around Joshua's neck as he had done so many times before. Joshua pulled Augustus to his feet and steadied the frail old man. Confident that Augustus was stable, Joshua stepped back, emitting a chuckle.

"Not quite the attire I would have expected of a great adventurer."

He looked at Augustus clad in an ankle-length nightshirt and slippers, the ensemble complete with stocking cap. Augustus replied with a laugh, "No, this is not quite how I envisioned it all these many years."

Augustus shuffled toward the large grandfather clock, Joshua holding his elbow and walking beside him. When they stood before the clock, Augustus turned, looked up at Joshua with a smile, and gave a slight nod. Joshua reached into his coat pocket and retrieved an ornately adorned golden key. He fit it into the keyhole of the large glass-paneled clock door, the result of which was the whirring of electricity and magnets as the tumblers clicked into alignment. With some effort, he opened the heavy door. For a moment, the two men admired the mechanism of the clock, the sound of which was much louder with the door opened. Joshua turned to Augustus. "After you, my friend." Augustus slowly entered the clock. Joshua cautioned, "Take care to avoid the pendulum, Augustus. A blow from that will end it here."

With that Joshua, too, entered the clock, pulled the door closed behind him, and locked it.

# CHAPTER 1

# Before Colchester

"Susan?"

As he entered her study and saw her, Scott realized that Susan was nowhere near being ready to leave. "Baby, if we don't leave soon, we're not going to make our flight. You know security for an international flight does take longer."

Susan responded without looking up from her desk, "I know. I'm almost ready. I just need to get through these last few calculations so I can shoot them over to Gelman. He's going to do some legwork while we're gone." Under her breath she added, "At least my work won't completely grind to a halt." With that, Susan adjusted her reading glasses to the end of her nose and continued laboring, with no apparent urgency.

Susan, an attractive woman of forty-two, did not fit the stereotypical mold of a quantum physicist. She was young, fit and very stylish. Nor did she match the stereotypical perception of the mother of two. Nevertheless, she was both. And she excelled at both. Dr. Susan Hawthorne was one of the most published and respected scientists in her field, and she rated "Pretty Cool Mom" with a very discerning committee of two: her children.

"I've got the kids' bags in the car. Are yours ready to be loaded?" Scott inserted himself into Susan's light in a deliberate, and successful, attempt to cast a distracting shadow upon her desk. Susan, not oblivious to his intention, laid her pencil upon the paper, removed her glasses and lifted her head to look at her husband. She couldn't help but smile because she knew him and his techniques so well. Scott was the perfect counterpart to Susan. They were complete opposites: Susan introspective and reserved, Scott extroverted and gregarious. Susan embedded in the disciplines of natural sciences, Scott, a novelist with a doctorate in history, at home in the liberal arts. It was their opposite natures that drew them together and kept them together, much like magnets attracted to opposite polarities. In two important aspects, however, they did not differ: their love for each other and their love for their children.

"Where are Livi and Jack?" asked Susan, relenting to Scott's persistence.

"Where else? Jack's in his room practicing magic and Livi's in her room reading a book," replied Scott.

"I should have guessed," laughed Susan. "I don't hear arguing."

Scott rounded the desk, sat opposite Susan and reached over to rest his hand upon her forearm. "Honey, this trip will be good for them. They'll be away from TV, video games, Facebook, their friends; they'll have only each other to entertain themselves. They'll have to get along. It'll be good for all of us. This is a once-in-a-lifetime opportunity. I for one am looking forward to it."

"Of course you're looking forward to it," responded Susan emphatically. "You're a historian traveling to one of the oldest boroughs in Great Britain. I, on the other hand, am sacrificing valuable time that should be spent on research. I don't know why we can't just let the executor obtain a broker and dispose of the property."

Three months previously Susan had been notified that she was the only surviving heir to the Hollingsworth estate. As such, she inherited Hollingsworth Manor in Colchester, England. Though Susan had known that she had some distant link to family in the UK, she had never met any of them and knew nothing of the reportedly years-vacant manor. As the sole heir, it fell upon her to either maintain the manor or dispose of it. She opted to dispose of it and, had she had her druthers, would have done so sight-unseen by way of a broker. Scott, however, insisted that they inspect the property, if for no other reason than to gain historical perspective on Susan's family. Susan now regretted having assented to the trip.

"It's going to be a great trip," said Scott consolingly. As he stood, he offered his hand in assistance. Susan regarded her handsome yet nerdy husband with a resigned smile, took his hand and stood as well. Together they headed off to corral their children and usher them to the waiting car.

Scott loaded the last of the luggage into the back of the mini-van and took note of his family as he eased his lanky frame into the driver's seat. "Come on guys, this is going to be a great adventure. I promise." Susan, in an effort to be a good sport, forced a smile and patted Scott on the leg.

As for the children behind them, it was a different story. Both sat crossed-armed and pouting, Livi because she was being jerked away from her friends, cell phone and books, and Jack because he was "being punished": there was no TV where they were going and he was not allowed to bring his Game Boy. And to add insult to injury, they were actually going to have to hang out with each other. Livi was appalled that she would even have to be with the "obnoxious little brat," much less rely upon him for companionship. Jack, in turn, was none too happy to be stuck with the "snooty bookworm" for a whole summer. What a waste of vacation! "This is so lame," was Livi's muffled response to Scott's enthusiasm. Jack merely grunted and poked his lower lip out a bit farther.

Livi, short for Olivia, was a petite 16-year-old caught up in the social life of high school. She was exceptionally intelligent and erudite. Her passion for reading was legendary and paled only in comparison to her aptitude for math, calculus to be precise. Entering her junior year of high school, Livi was to take calculus-based physics and was actually looking forward to it. Despite her scholastic prowess, she was a well-rounded young woman. Her small frame suited her well for competitive gymnastics and cheerleading. She also was a starter for the girl's varsity soccer team. She thrived in her network of friends and spent countless hours communicating via text message and Facebook.

Jack, on the other hand, was not so academically oriented. As a 13-year-old going into eighth grade he, too, had a solid network of friends. But his love of school was predicated upon its social aspect. Jack, though also intelligent, didn't particularly care for all of that "book stuff." He did what he needed in order to get by. Jack's talents resided in the arts. He was a musician, a dancer, an actor and, most of all, an aspiring magician. He practiced magic for hours on end, much to the aggravation of Livi. He participated in team sports, but only because his friends did so. Jack preferred challenges of personal physical achievement, ergo his passion for rock climbing. Despite his gregarious personality, Jack was plagued by thoughts of self-doubt and inadequacy. In a family of academically oriented over-achievers, he felt well out of place. If not for the fact that he looked exactly like his father, he would be certain that he was adopted. In fact, didn't Livi often tell him that?

# CHAPTER 2

# Colchester

The Hawthornes arrived at London's Stansted Airport in the late morning. They grabbed a quick snack at a small deli inside the airport and proceeded to the car rental desk. After what seemed an eternity to Livi and Jack, they finally loaded their gear into the back of the silver Peugeot Wagon that Scott had rented. They had shipped the majority of their provisions ahead of time and were assured by the executor, Barrister Franklin, that they had arrived in good condition and had been delivered to Hollingsworth Manor.

Livi and Jack piled into the back seat of the car while Scott took the driver's seat, right side of course, and Susan the front passenger's seat. Scott was elated to have the opportunity to drive on the left side of the road. In fact, he had been practicing at home, much to the consternation of his neighbors and one nonplused police officer, who found no merit in Scott's reasoning and dutifully wrote a ticket. But it was of no matter to Scott now. He was in the mecca of history and in one hour would arrive in Colchester, the place upon which Emperor Claudius founded the Roman Province of Britannia. He would be at home in Colchester. Students from around the world came to study at the University of Essex. A stroll through the town center reportedly would expose one to a plethora of languages: French, Spanish, Dutch, Chinese and Italian, to name a few. What a great place to reflect and research and write! Scott was giddy with excitement.

The others...not so much. Livi was outraged that they couldn't drive the thirty minutes in the other direction to London to see important sites--like Harrods. Susan was miffed because she had been cut off in mid-sentence with a distraught Gelman regarding some research funding issue, by a regimented stewardess who insisted "all electronic devices must be turned to the off position, Ma'am."

Jack, he was tired. He didn't know what he was going to do for the hour drive. But then it hit him. "Dad, wait! I need to get my magic set."

Livi, who had just started to read her copy of Charles Dickens' Oliver Twist (summer reading list), slammed it down on her knee. "Mom, don't let that little freak start with that magic stuff." She turned to Jack and snarled, "Stay put, you little weirdo."

"Well, what else am I going to do for an hour, talk to you?" Jack retorted.

Livi, seeing that as a more severe alternative, relented her stand. "Fine, whatever."

Scott eased the car onto the shoulder of the road and Jack unbuckled his seat belt. He leaned over the seat and accessed his small magic kit. From it emerged a rope and a pamphlet of instructions. Once settled back in place, he refastened his belt and the Hawthornes embarked upon their journey.

Livi, well into her reading forty-five minutes into the drive, was shocked back to reality by Jack's sudden and vociferous outburst. "Whoa, that is so cool! Livi, tie me up."

Livi looked at Jack with incredulousness. "What? Shut up, I'm reading."

"Come on, just one time," Jack persisted. "I want to see if I can make it work."

Not one to give in easily, Livi graciously declined the invitation. "Go away, jerk, I don't want to play with your pathetic little magic tricks."

Susan, having heard enough of this conversation, reprimanded Livi. "Livi, be polite. If you don't want to do something, say so nicely. There is no reason to talk to your brother like that." Jack protruded his tongue and then mouthed silently to Livi, "Yeah, jerk."

Livi responded with a hint of sarcasm, "Thank you, dear brother, but I don't care to partake in your fanciful feats of illusion."

Jack was not appeased and pleaded his case to his father with only one word: "Daaad?" A touch exacerbated himself with the exchange, Scott came to the rescue. "Livi, would it be so hard to do just one thing with your brother?"

As though the answer was obvious, Livi replied, "Yeah! I mean, after all what's the point? It's not like that's an important life skill. It's just like that stupid rock climbing he does." She turned her attention to Jack. "You're really going to make a great living doing that," Livi said sarcastically.

Jack responded with indignation, "Hey, I hold the record for the fastest time on the rock wall!"

Livi dryly replied, "I'm so impressed."

"Livi, everyone has different talents and different skills. Jack is going to do just fine. You need to be a little more tolerant and open-minded," said Scott.

Susan echoed his sentiments, addressing Jack: "Honey, everyone has a role in life. You don't have to have the same interests as anybody else. Do the best you can in the areas that are required, like school, and follow your passion. That's how one becomes successful in life. We just want you both to be happy."

Livi rolled her eyes and shook her head. Scott, noting this in the mirror, cautioned her: "Livi?"

Seeing her father's disapproving glance in the rear view mirror, Livi amended her response. "Fine. What do you want me to do, freako?"

Jack enthusiastically instructed Livi to tie the rope around his wrists and stated that he would set himself free. So, Livi did just that, and none too gently. After she had ensured, at Jack's request, that the binding was secure, Jack spoke the magic words: "Livi stinks!" and the rope fell away from his wrists.

Jack glanced proudly at Livi in light of his triumph. He was rewarded with a "Humph," as Livi resumed reading. She wasn't about to let Jack know that she was, in fact, duly impressed. Why didn't he put forth the same effort towards reading and schoolwork? She truly was worried about his future, even though her mom and dad didn't see that.

Jack appeared to return his attention to the instruction booklet. In truth, he was deep in thought, disturbed by the exchange that had just occurred. He always became unsettled when conversation turned towards his goals and aspirations, or more so the lack thereof. Jack felt like an outsider in his family. He really didn't know where he fit. He wasn't at all interested in reading and science like his mom and sister. And, unlike his dad, he didn't care much for history either. He liked to perform. Whether acting, playing music, performing magic or even rock climbing, he thrived on the attention it brought. And he was good at those things. He did hold the rock wall record, after all. Not only that; he could set up all of the rigging to climb a rock wall, and at age thirteen, he was already certified to belay others. That was something, right? Jack could play drums and piano and he was always the lead in school plays. That was good, wasn't it? Still, Jack feared that Livi was right. Where would all of that get him in life? He didn't know, and it was starting to bother him. Jack tried to push these thoughts from his mind and focus his attention on the magic set. He was unsuccessful.

Soon thereafter the Hawthornes rolled into Colchester, having taken the scenic London Road rather than the motorway. At the traffic circle of Colne Bank Avenue, Cowdray Avenue and North Station Road, Scott turned right. Of course he should have gone left around the circle instead, which he realized when Susan braced herself against the dash, simultaneously depressing the nonexistent brake at her feet. Scott had not quite yet mastered driving in the UK. Nevertheless, he made it onto North Station Road and the family proceeded to Culver Street West, where they turned left. There they encountered the north range of the enormous fifteenth-century timber-framed house on the right that was Hollingsworth Manor.

Scott slowed the car to a crawl as he drove alongside the house. "This is it, Susan," he declared. Susan could only nod in affirmation as she marveled at the house.

"Whoa, that's it?" queried Jack. Livi could only stare in wonderment. If her friends could see this place they would be "sooo jealous." "Does it have a pool?" Jack pressed.

Hollingsworth Manor was composed of three distinct "ranges." In effect, these were three different houses assembled into a whole. As was the mode of the day, the fifteenth-century home was constructed in stages, allowing the owners of the house to reside in the first constructed range while the remaining structures were built. The north range was the first to be built and was oriented along its length parallel to Culver Street West. This structure, like the remaining two ranges, was two and a half stories in height and was covered with a tiled gable roof. The second story, after the custom of timber-framed construction, was "jetted" above the first, meaning that its outer walls extended beyond the walls of the first story in an overhanging manner. The breastworks of two stone-constructed fireplaces were proportionately stacked against the side of the wooden structure. The chimneys, which provided common draft for fireboxes on each of the three interior floors, extended well above the peaks of the roof. Large shuttered windows extended across both the first and second stories. Dormers jutted out from the roof of the upper half-story.

Scott continued to drive slowly, making the right turn onto Trinity, which brought the family to the front of the manor. The front range of the house was perpendicular to and set back from the north and south ranges. A large double door and transom were the focal point of the house. Floor-length windows extended from either side of the massive doorway and opened onto a stone gallery that ran the length of the eastward-facing middle range. The manor was set back from the street upon a mound. A four-foot stone retaining wall ran parallel and adjacent to the walkway that serviced Trinity. It was within this wall that a gate opened onto a gravel drive that circled in front of the house. Windows and dormers occupied the second and upper levels of the house respectively. Two chimneys could be seen rising from the back of the middle range. The south range, which was to the left as one faced the house, was a mirror image of the north range.

Scott slowly drove around the entire block that the property occupied. When he returned to the front of the manor he stopped the car. Scott turned off the engine and stepped out of the Peugeot. His family followed suit. "Susan, this is beautiful," he said. Susan nodded assent, "It is that." And it was.

Jack opened the low gate and began to walk toward the house. He paused when he noted that none of the others followed. "Well, come on, let's go in," he said as he turned to eye his family.

"Can't, dufus," Livi informed him.

Susan clarified, "We don't have the key, baby. Mr. Franklin isn't going to meet us here for another couple of hours."

Jack was disheartened. "Oh man. Well, I'm going to take a look." He ran up the drive and jumped onto the gallery, bypassing the three steps that were conventionally used. He cupped his hands around his eyes and pressed his nose to the large window next to the front door, peering inside. After a moment he announced, "It's huge!" Jack turned, jumped down from the gallery and began to walk back. "All the furniture is covered," he said.

"The house has been vacant for years, Jack," said Scott. "We'll check it out when we get back. Come on guys, I've got a treat for you while we wait. We're going to a castle!"

Scott, hand in hand with Susan, began walking toward the High Street. Jack ran up enthusiastically to join them. "A real castle? Here? Cool!" Jack was elated.

Livi was aghast. "We're going to a castle? How lame. And we're walking? You've got to be kidding me. It's a hundred degrees out here!"

Without turning or stopping, Susan offered hope. "It's only a couple of blocks. It won't kill you." And off they went, Livi lagging behind in protest.

# CHAPTER 3

# Colchester Castle

Colchester Castle is an imposing stone structure. It is in fact the largest Norman keep in Europe. The castle, built upon the ruins of the Roman Temple of Claudius, was completed in 1101 A.D., some thirty years after its construction began. Scott eagerly shared this information as the castle came into view. His audience was less than captivated.

"Whoa, this is so cool," was Jack's response, as he stood next to the front wall and craned his neck back to peer at the upper limits of the structure.

Upon approach to Colchester Castle, one notes that the main entryway, which is serviced by a footbridge that allows access to its elevated position, is situated off-center to the left. Jagged reddish-brown faded stone makes up the exterior of the massive structure. The face of the castle is adorned with two small arched windows on the lower level and three large arched windows on the upper. Square towers are situated at each corner, yet on the right side stands a larger rounded tower. Situated upon the left-facing tower is a domed precipice, which marks the apogee of the castle. Jack strained to make out the image upon the flag mounted at its top.

As the Hawthornes entered the museum, they stood momentarily in the cool of the keep to allow their eyes to adjust from the outdoor brightness to the dim interior lighting. They took the opportunity to absorb the enormity of the structure and refresh themselves after the heat of the outdoors. Scott was in heaven: two thousand years of British history assembled in one place. He was like a kid in a toyshop. With the grin of a Cheshire cat, Scott addressed Livi: "What do you think?"

"This is really neat," Livi had to admit, despite her efforts to be unimpressed.

Susan walked over to the information desk and grabbed up four brochures detailing the exhibits available for viewing in the museum. She instructed her family as she presented a pamphlet to each. "Okay guys, we have about two hours. Let's all meet back here by 3:00 p.m." As Jack moved away from the group, Livi instructed him, "Don't go touching everything. I don't want to get thrown out of here because of you." Susan yet again reminded Livi: "Jack has very capable parents. You worry about yourself. Now, you two go have fun."

With that, Jack darted off. Livi rolled her eyes, turned and walked away, opening her brochure as she did so. "Fine," was her muted response, though in fact, she was looking forward to the exploration.

As the children wandered off, Susan took Scott's hand as he stood perusing his options. In a tone more matronly than she had intended, Susan asked, "Well, what would you like to see first? And remember, we'll be here all summer so you don't have to see it all today."

Scott replied with a childlike glint in his eye, "Let's start at the beginning. We'll go to the Roman exhibit." Hand in hand, Scott and Susan walked into the dim recesses of the keep.

Livi, having long ago lost sight of Jack, proceeded to the English Literature exhibit. A presentation on Beowulf caught her attention, as she had read the tenth-century work the previous spring semester. She briefly scanned Chaucer's The Canterbury Tales, breezed through a treatise on Shakespeare and other sixteenth-century authors, paused at John Milton's Paradise Lost, marveled at a biography of Jane Austen, and was stopped dead in her tracks by an exhibit on her favored author of the Victorian Age, Charles Dickens. Livi was drawn to the exposé presented on Dickens' Oliver Twist. After all, what better way to gain insight for her report that would be due when she returned to school? Dickens, as a newcomer on the literary scene, wrote this piece as an encore to his popular comedy, The Pickwick Papers. The work was published in monthly installments in <u>Bentley's Miscellany</u>, as was the mode of the day, between February 1837 and April 1839. Livi read with intent interest the social conditions of the early Victorian era that provided fodder for Dickens' work. She cringed at the images and descriptions of the workhouses to which poor and orphaned children were subjected. She became angry upon learning of the brutal and dangerous apprenticeships children were made to endure. She so wanted to know more of Dickens, the man who exposed such atrocities of social oppression.

As Livi delved into Dickens' biography, she was fascinated to learn that he had actually resided in Colchester. Dickens, as a young man desirous of becoming a reporter, taught himself shorthand. At the age of sixteen, he became a court reporter. By 1834, at the age of 22, Dickens had become a journalist covering Parliamentary debate, and traveled across Britain covering election campaigns for the <u>Morning Chronicle</u>. In 1835, he was reporting in Colchester. Livi laughed when she read that he reported under the pseudonym Boz. What a silly name for such a serious man, she thought. Livi did not move from the Dickens exhibit until retrieved to meet her family.

Jack, meanwhile, proceeded to the ground floor of the castle, where he stumbled across an exhibit on the history of "Colchester Castle and its Witches." At first, he was thrilled with the prospect of reading accounts of witches and their works of magic. But as he read, he became rather morose. There were no fanciful tales of sorcery. There was no mention of Merlin. No magical rescue of a damsel in distress. There wasn't even the smallest reference to Harry Potter. Wasn't he the most famous wizard of Britain? Instead, he found tales of sorrow and wretchedness.

Colchester Castle was the site of seventeenth-century witch trials. Jack read of the elderly, the crippled, the poor and the misfits being accused of witchcraft for no reason other than that they were easy targets. He read of the mentality of fear that prompted the villagers to accuse one other in an effort to prevent being accused themselves, and how persons wrongfully accused were held prisoner in this very castle. Jack read with loathing of the account of one Matthew Hopkins, the self-proclaimed Witchfinder General, who conducted witch trials right here in Colchester Castle. Jack learned how Hopkins extorted large amounts of silver from the citizens of the counties of East Anglia to "rid" each town of witches. Hopkins extracted confessions from the weak and infirm through torture. He masterminded convictions and carried out death sentences right here on the castle grounds. Jack learned of the tools Hopkins used to prove a person was a witch. In the seventeenth century, it was believed that if a witch was bound and thrown into the water, he or she would float because the water, as the instrument of baptism, would reject the witch. Hopkins would perform this "swim test" in the River Colne, the very river that ran behind the castle. The victim was bound by the hands to a wooden boom that extended over the river. He would order the "witch" dipped into the water and at the moment before drowning, the accused would somehow rise back to the surface, proving that he or she was a witch. Jack struggled to understand how that could possibly happen, as he read on about the "Devil's Mark." Purportedly, if a witch's skin were pierced, the witch would not bleed. Jack read that Hopkins, after days of torturing the accused, would thrust a knife into his or her body. The result was always the same, no stab mark or bleeding, proving the accused to be a witch.

Again, Jack pondered this incredulously. He read for over an hour the accounts of Matthew Hopkins, and had only some small sense of justice in learning that in the end, Hopkins was exposed by a local preacher, John Gaule. Here accounts differed. Some claimed that Hopkins was arrested and ultimately subjected to the same atrocities that he imposed upon others, resulting in Hopkins' execution by hanging. Others claimed that Hopkins went into seclusion, ultimately dying an old man, of tuberculosis. For a boy of reputed carefree attitude, Jack found himself quite unsettled by what he learned in Colchester Castle this day.

# CHAPTER 4

# The Manor House

At the appointed time the Hawthorne family reported back to the reception area of Colchester Castle. All except for Livi, that is, who had to be retrieved by her father from her historical introduction to Charles Dickens. The family emerged from the cool confines of the keep into the muggy air of coastal, summertime Colchester. They hiked back to Hollingsworth Manor, where they found waiting Barrister James Franklin, an elderly man of short stature and expanded girth, who stood in dignified posture, if such is possible for a man of such morphology. Franklin, as a member of the Honourable Society of Middle Temple, had some years ago joined the set of Chambers that had provided legal counsel for the Hollingsworth estate for well over a century. As executor of the estate, it was his duty to assist the heir of the estate in legal matters. With that solemn duty in mind, Franklin approached the last living Hollingsworth heir and extended a pudgy hand.

"Dr. Hawthorne, this is indeed an immense pleasure. I am your most humble servant, James Franklin. We have corresponded."

"Barrister Franklin, it is very nice to meet you," replied Susan, as she received the handshake. "Thank you so much for helping us." Susan removed her hand from Franklin's grip, moving it to touch Scott on the sleeve. "This is my husband Scott and our children, Olivia and Jack."

"Sir, indeed a pleasure," said Franklin with a handshake and a slight bow. Then, turning to Livi, he took her hand and touched it to his lips. "What a lovely young lady. I am honored." Livi nodded a greeting and as Franklin turned his attention to Jack, she turned to her mother, rolled her eyes and wiped her hand on the back of her jeans. Susan returned that with a stern expression and a slight shake of the head.

"And you, young man, are quite the tiger, I see," Franklin said as he pumped Jack's hand.

Not really sure how to reply, Jack merely said, "Thank you."

When Franklin returned his attention to Susan, Jack looked at his dad and shrugged his shoulders. Scott responded with a wink and a smile, causing a grin to emerge upon Jack's face.

"Now Dr. Hawthorne, are you quite sure you want to stay in the house? I can procure a lovely room at the Swallow George. It's just next over on the High Street.

I'm certain that we can have this matter executed in due time."

Scott, knowing what Franklin suggested was exactly what Susan would prefer, intervened. "Thank you, Mr. Franklin, but our hearts are set on staying in the house. We're looking forward to exploring Susan's family roots."

"Yes, of course," said Franklin with just a hint of disdain.

"I presume that the house is in good order?" asked Scott.

"As per Dr. Hawthorne's instructions, I have had the engineers see to it that all is in good repair. As you know, Lord Hollingsworth bequeathed a trust to maintain and modernize the manor house," answered Franklin. "I'm afraid that since no one has lived in the house for decades, the last plumbing, gas, and electrical upgrades predate the Second World War. As you can imagine, some work was required in anticipation of your arrival."

"Well then, looks like everything is set. Let's take a look," said Scott.

"Yeah!" endorsed Jack as he once again ran up the drive to the door.

"Very good, sir, as you wish." Franklin turned toward the house as he retrieved a key from his pocket. With a deep breath, he led the others to the house, climbed the three steps that had yet to support Jack's feet, and inserted the key into the tumbler of the massive front double door. Franklin opened the door and stepped aside, making room for the family to enter. Jack shot in and disappeared into the house like a bolt of lightning. Livi, Susan and Scott entered behind, followed by Barrister Franklin who, with some deliberation, made sure that the door stayed open.

The front door of the manor opened into a large stone-floored entryway. To the immediate left was a sitting area that had served as the evening parlor. As one faced the parlor, large ceiling-to-floor length windows opened onto the front gallery to the left. Straight ahead was a set of double doors that accessed a room behind. To the right was a wall that curved slightly back into the morning parlor, to the right of the entryway. It was the mirror image of the evening parlor, with the exception that it communicated directly with a large open room that served as a breakfast and informal dining room. The Hawthornes' boxed possessions, which had been previously shipped, were arranged within the two parlors. Straight ahead as one entered the house was a large open stairway that tiered to the second level. Behind and through the stairway one could see the expansive room that functioned as the ballroom, banquet hall and formal dining area. This area was open from the floor to the ceiling of the second story. A second-floor gallery surrounded and looked into the large room from above. Two fireplaces occupied the back wall of this room, which opened onto a large courtyard behind the house. As Jack had noted earlier, all of the furnishings were draped.

Franklin directed attention to the breakfast room. "Perhaps we can retire in here to discuss the disposal of the property." He led the way through the morning parlor into the breakfast room and pulled a drape from the large table, exposing it and its accompanying chairs. "I apologize for all of the furniture draping, I shall have someone over this evening to remove and store them." With that, he set his attaché upon the table and extracted a collection of papers from within. "Please sit," he said as he gestured to Susan, Scott and Livi to take seats, Jack having yet to re-emerge.

Livi considered a moment, decided that this discussion was not likely to be of great interest, and excused herself. "I think I'm going to take a look around." She turned and walked back toward the entryway. "Be careful, baby," cautioned Scott.

Livi walked to the stairway and began her tiered ascent. As she neared the top, Jack came bounding down. "This place is awesome!" he said as he darted past Livi on his way to the first floor. At the top of the stairs, Livi found herself on the railed gallery that formed a square looking down into the massive ballroom. She turned left and started walking. Livi opened a door to her immediate left and found it to be a bedroom. As she made the right turn heading toward the back of the house, she encountered another door. This opened into a large study that was adjoined to an upper parlor at the front of the house. These two rooms occupied the entirety of the second story of the south range. She continued on to the back of the gallery, which opened along its length in three places onto a balcony that overlooked the rear courtyard. As she again turned right and made her way toward the front of the house, she encountered the large master suite that occupied the entire second story of the north range of the manor. Livi turned yet again and saw a second bedroom at the front of the house that mirrored the room on the other side of the stairway. She turned and leaned against the railing overlooking the ballroom. She realized she had never seen anything like this before. As she peered down, she could imagine herself the princess at an elegant ball. She and her escort, dancing to the waltz of a chamber quartet, just like Cinderella and the Prince. That was a life she could certainly get used to. The echo of Jack's voice reverberating "hello!" shattered Livi's reverie.

Jack had returned to the first floor and entered the breakfast room, announcing to its occupants once again, "This place is so cool!" He entered the kitchen, which was off the back wall of the breakfast room. He found it to be rather smaller than he would have expected for such a big house. Two doors were situated on the back wall of the kitchen, and he spent a good deal of time exploring what both revealed. The door to the right opened into small suite that had a sitting area and a partition concealing a sleeping area. He presumed a manor this extensive would have servants, and correctly concluded that this was the servants' quarters. The door to the left opened into a large walk-in pantry that in turn opened onto the back courtyard, which he briefly reconnoitered. As he returned through the pantry back into the kitchen, he encountered another door that opened into the large ballroom. Jack entered the ballroom and noted its expansiveness. He walked toward the middle of the room and peered up to the ceiling of the second story. As he pivoted in place, he noticed Livi looking over the rail. "Hello!" called Jack, listening for the echo. Livi, startled by the sudden outburst, was none too happy. "Quit yelling, jerk!"

Jack laughed as he began to make his way to the other side of the room. Livi turned and headed back down the stairs. When Jack reached the south wall of the ballroom, he encountered a set of mahogany double doors. He grasped both handles and pulled the two doors open into the ballroom. Jack entered the dark room before him, turned and pulled the doors shut. He made his way across the room toward where sunlight peeked out from behind the thick draperies covering a window on the opposite wall. After negotiating his way through the maze of massive covered obstacles, upon one of which he stubbed his large toe, he successfully reached the window and pulled the drapes open. With the room now adequately illuminated, he turned to take in his surroundings. What he saw astounded him.

Livi returned to the breakfast room where she saw Scott, Susan and Mr. Franklin poring over bundles of papers that had been spread across the table. Livi took a seat next to her mother.

"Mr. Franklin, it appears to me that other houses of comparable size have sold for much more than what we are asking," noted Susan. "And yet you say that there has been only one serious offer?"

"Yes madam, I'm afraid that is true," responded Franklin. "The gentleman who has made the offer is an Indian businessman. He has offered to buy the manor as is for the price stipulated."

"Why is he willing to buy the property?" asked Scott.

"He wishes to make a development," replied Franklin.

"I beg your pardon?" responded Scott, not quite understanding.

"This gentleman is a commercial real estate developer," said Franklin. "He intends to level the house and build a shopping centre upon the property."

"Tear down this manor?" asked Susan.

"I'm afraid so," sighed Franklin.

"Mr. Franklin, surely a house this old has some historical significance that would preclude it being demolished," retorted Scott. He then directed his attention to Susan. "I'm sure if we invest a little to restore the property, more suitable buyers with an eye toward preservation will come forward."

"Dr. Hawthorne, the town commission has given indication that they will allow for the destruction of this house and the construction of a shopping centre," Franklin disclosed.

"That would be insane!" said Susan. "Why would anyone allow that?"

Franklin looked down at his hands for a moment before raising his glance to Susan. "Dr. Hawthorne, there is more to this issue than the fact that the manor is in some disrepair," confessed Franklin. He continued, "This property, in some form, has been in the Hollingsworth family since the Middle Ages. Since the fifteenth century, this house has been present on the property. The last resident of the manor was Lord Jonathan William Augustus Hollingsworth IV. Augustus was a rather eccentric man. As a young man, he became fascinated with timepieces. His father, to placate Augustus' passion, had him apprenticed to the local clockmaker, Samuel Downum. Samuel learned his craft from the most famous Colchester clockmaker, John Smorthwaite."

Scott interjected, "Augustus was a noble. How is it that he would be apprenticed to a clockmaker? And what does any of this have to do with the manor?"

"It is a bit complicated," Franklin admitted. "Augustus was trained privately here at the manor; his apprenticeship was not registered. Even so, he was a member of the Worshipful Company of Clockmakers." Franklin continued, "In every room of this house are numerous timepieces, large and small, almost all of them constructed by Augustus."

"So this guy was nuts about clocks. Again, what does that have to do with the lack of interest in the manor?" asked Susan.

Franklin pressed on. "Augustus lived in the manor all of his life. Shortly after his marriage, Augustus' wife died, leaving no heirs. Augustus never remarried. He lived in the house with his manservant and continued to make clocks. In 1896, both Augustus and his servant disappeared. They were never seen again."

"I still don't get the connection," said Scott.

"Dr. Hawthorne, it is rumored that this manor is haunted by Augustus Hollingsworth."

"Haunted? Is that why no one is interested in the house?" asked Susan incredulously. "Surely no one believes that?"

"There have been unexplained phenomena that lend credence to the thought," said Franklin sheepishly. "One of Augustus' clocks, a rather large grandfather clock in the library, continues to run. All of the others have stopped." Franklin paused. "The clock appears to be wound every week, yet no one has the key to access the mechanism."

In the silence that followed while Susan and Scott tried to register this information, Jack's voice rang out. "Livi!"

Jack surveyed the library with his mouth agape. He had never seen anything like this in his life. In fact, the only thing that came close was the library of the Beast's castle depicted in Disney's Beauty and the Beast. The library with its oak floor extended the entire length of the south range of the manor. The outer wall of the room was adorned with tall windows covered with dense satin drapes the color of crimson. Between the windows were mahogany bookshelves that rose to within three feet of the fifteen-foot, corniced ceiling. Oriented in the center of this wall was the largest fireplace Jack had ever seen. He walked toward it and entered the firebox, stepping between the rods of the grate. He noted that someone twice his height could easily enter without stooping. As he stepped out, he noted that the remaining three walls were likewise lined with similar bookshelves. No area of bare wall was exposed. Each shelf of each case was filled to overflowing with books of every size. Large wheeled ladders on rails serviced each section of book casings. "Livi is going to go nuts," Jack thought aloud.

But what fascinated him most was the object directly across the room from the fireplace. It was only as he eyed this object that he became aware of the source of the metronome-like ticking that he'd registered when he entered the room. In front of him, buttressed by the now familiar book casings, was an enormous grandfather clock that extended to the ceiling. The clock was as wide as he was tall and was fronted by a large opaque-glassed door that, presumably, led to the mechanism.

"Whoa!" Jack said aloud. "Livi has got to see this." Seeing the second set of double doors that led to the evening parlor, Jack hurried to open them as he excitedly called for his sister. "Livi!"

Barrister Franklin, anxious to leave the manor before dark, made his exit after walking through the property with the Hawthornes. He had pointed out numerous features of the house, but admitted that he did not know it well. Scott assured him that discovery of the house would be part of the adventure. He convinced Mr. Franklin that it would not be necessary to send a crew to uncover the furniture; he and his family were more than capable.

It was also decided, much to Franklin's dismay, that Susan would not sell the house to anyone who intended to demolish it. She and Scott were willing to spend the money and time, the whole summer if necessary, to refurbish the manor in preparation for sale to a suitable candidate. Susan dismissed the idea of the manor being haunted by Augustus Hollingsworth, stating that there was some logical explanation for the functioning of the clock and that she would reveal its secret in due time.

As Franklin drove off, the Hawthornes got down to the business of moving in. "Okay guys, let's unload the car first, then we can tackle the boxes," suggested Scott. The family progressed to the Peugeot wagon, which was parked on the circular drive in front of the house. Scott issued orders as he began pulling bags from within the car.

"Let's see, Jack. Here is your magic kit, climbing gear and travel bag. These go to your room. Livi, here are your books and travel bag for your room. And the rest are for Mom and I to take to our room. Everyone meet back downstairs and we'll start unpacking boxes, uncovering furniture and cleaning up. We've got a lot of work to do to get this place presentable."

Livi and Jack dutifully gathered their gear and headed toward the house, bantering as they went. "Why did you bring all of that stupid climbing gear? Where do you think you're going to be able to climb?" asked Livi as they walked.

"You never know when it might come in handy," replied Jack. "Why did you bring two bags of books? It's not like the library doesn't have more books than you could read in a lifetime."

"I didn't know about the library, dufus," retorted Livi.

The kids meandered their way up the stairs and parted ways at the top. Livi took the bedroom to the left of the stairs, stating that it made more sense for her to be by the study. Jack acquiesced to the bedroom right of the stairs. Livi suggested that to be his best option so he could be close to "mommy" if the ghost of Augustus scared him. Jack assured her that he did not believe in ghosts, although the thought had occupied his mind since learning of Franklin's story of the clock. Truth be told, being close to his parents comforted him. Of course, he would never admit that to Livi.

Jack opened the door to his room and entered. He placed his climbing gear and magic kit on top of his draped bed and set his travel bag upon the floor. He took a moment to survey his new domain and uncovered the bedside table, taking care not to topple the lamp. "This room is better than Livi's anyway." With that decided, Jack headed back downstairs.

The Hawthornes spent the next few hours busy at work. Susan suggested that they work on the two parlors, the breakfast area and kitchen, saving the rest of the downstairs for the following day. She intentionally avoided the library, knowing that Scott and Livi would be of no use once they got in there. Instead, she sent them to begin work in the breakfast room while she and Jack tackled the kitchen, servants' quarters, and ballroom. The two teams worked well, rapidly uncovering and dusting the furniture, moving boxes and storing away provisions.

As the night waned, Susan realized that they had not had anything to eat since leaving the castle museum earlier that day. "Jack, how's it going in there?" Susan asked.

Jack, who was stocking the pantry, called out through the open door, "Just about done."

Susan then opened the door from the kitchen into the breakfast room. "You guys getting hungry?" she queried Scott and Livi.

"I am, actually," responded Scott.

"Baby, will you run and get the box of paper plates?" Susan asked Livi. "I'll make some sandwiches. We can start up again tomorrow."

"Sure, Mom," Livi said.

Livi jumped down from the chair that she had been using as a step stool and set her dusting cloth upon the table. She went out into the morning parlor in search of the designated box. As she traversed the entryway, she noted Jack's feet as he bounded up the last spiral of the stairs. What Livi didn't notice was that the door to the library was ajar. She located the box of paper plates, which was grouped with others in the evening parlor.

She gathered it up and brought it to her mom in the kitchen.

"Thank you, baby," said Susan. "Now, do you want ham or turkey?"

"I'll take turkey," answered Livi.

"Jack, do you want ham or turkey?" Susan called into the pantry.

Jack answered as he emerged, "I'll have turkey too." Livi, somewhat puzzled, addressed Jack, "Where did you come from?"

Gesturing over his shoulder with his thumb toward the pantry, Jack answered the obvious: "From there."

"But you were just upstairs," stated Livi.

"What?" responded Jack, a bit confused.

Just then, Scott entered. "I'll have ham," he declared. Livi, now distracted, did not pursue her questioning of Jack.

The Hawthornes sat at the breakfast table and ate quietly. They were exhausted yet content. They discussed plans for the next day, and determined that they would finish with the downstairs in the morning and move to straightening the upstairs in the afternoon. Sometime during the day, they would have to make a run to the market. Once everything was stored away, they would start working on repairs inside the house. They would save the exterior refurbishment for last.

With the day done, the family headed upstairs to their respective bedrooms. At the top of the stairs, they bid each other good night and parted ways. Truly exhausted,

Jack opened the door to his room and entered. He pushed the top button of the old switch on the wall next to the doorway that turned on the overhead light. He then walked over to the lamp on the bedside table. He was happy to find that the lamp worked when he turned the switch. He then swept the drape off his bed and bundled it onto the floor. He was happy to see that the bed had what appeared to be comfortable linens. He opened his travel bag, pulled out his toiletries and pajamas and headed for the bathroom. He hit the bottom button of the wall switch on his way out, turning off the overhead light. It did not register with him that his magic kit and climbing gear were not on the bed where he had earlier placed them.

# CHAPTER 5

# Livi Makes a Discovery

Over the ensuing weeks, the Hawthornes made significant progress in refurbishing the manor. Occasionally, Scott and Susan would contract help in the project, electrical and plumbing for instance, but for the most part they did the interior work themselves. Livi and Jack, initially out of boredom, also helped. Ultimately they became invested in the undertaking, developing a true appreciation for the house. What's more, in the course of events they discovered that it wasn't so bad being together. Though they wouldn't openly admit it (or perhaps they didn't even realize it), Livi and Jack came to enjoy each other's companionship. Certainly, Scott and Susan noticed, but from fear of jinxing the development, they kept the observation to themselves.

As work on the interior of the house began to wind down, the Hawthornes found time to explore Colchester and the surrounding areas. They had already been to London twice, on both occasions making the foray to

Harrods, much to Livi's delight. And they had spent considerable time in the countryside visiting nearby villages. Mostly they discovered Colchester, becoming quite familiar with the town and its inhabitants. They came to appreciate the town not only for its historical significance, but also for the friendliness and diversity of its people. The locals were always fascinated to learn that the Hawthornes were living in Hollingsworth Manor. Despite Susan and Scott's assertions to the contrary, the locals continued in their belief that the manor was haunted. Susan and Scott assured them that they had seen no evidence that Augustus Hollingsworth's spirit was on the premises.

It was true that the grandfather clock in the library of the manor did become wound every week. It was also true that Susan was unable to divine an explanation for the phenomenon. Some brief thought was given to dismantling the door of the clock, but that was quickly dismissed in light of the damage that surely would result. Perhaps in the future, they could find a locksmith to create a key to access the inner workings of the clock. In any event, Susan explained that she was confident that Augustus had devised a mechanism to wind the clock and that once the device was revealed, the rumors of haunting would dissipate. As it stood, however, another issue was more pressing. Scott and Susan were struggling to find a qualified carpenter to restore the exterior structure of the fifteenth-century manor. Before they could seriously entertain prospective buyers, the work would have to be completed. They would tackle the mystery of the clock later.

The Hawthorne family took many excursions to the local attractions of Colchester. Jack's favorite destination remained the castle's museum. He became fascinated not only with the exhibits, but also with the history of the castle itself. Jack became friendly with the curator of the museum and learned much of its undocumented history. He got to know every square foot of the castle in its current state and was familiar with how it had changed over the centuries. Jack was sure that he knew more about castles than anyone else in Colchester, except for the curator of course. He certainly knew more than anyone from his town in the States. Of course, he wasn't sure how that would serve him in the future. He doubted that one could make a living as a castle expert. Why was it that none of his interests seemed to lend themselves to a secure livelihood?

Thinking of his interests reminded him that he needed to find a climbing shop to get more gear. Despite all of the boxes being unpacked, he was unable to find the bag of rock-climbing gear and the magic set that he had put on his bed that first day. He suspected that Livi had confiscated them, but she asserted that she had not. No one had seen the items in question.

Susan, much to her relief, was able to resume her research, at least in a limited sense. She was granted a courtesy appointment at the University of Essex in Colchester and had use of the physics library. She made sure to communicate with Gelman via the university email system at least twice weekly. Scott was thrilled to be anywhere in Colchester. He too had access to the university libraries, but found the town itself to be a historical resource and a font of inspiration for his works of fiction.

Though Livi too enjoyed the excursions into town and the surrounding areas, she was happiest in the manor. She spent countless hours in the massive library, scouring through the vast collection of books. Jack was right, when Livi first saw the library, she did go nuts. Livi would roll the ladders across the shelves and study all of the titles. Most times she would take a book and plant herself in one of the oversized chairs to read. It was not uncommon for her to complete a book in a single sitting. Sometimes she would begin to peruse the book while standing on the ladder, and become so engrossed that she would complete the reading there. At night, when she was supposed to be asleep, she would sneak into the upstairs study and read the books contained therein. It was during one of these late-night forays that she made the most amazing discovery.

"Dad and I have to go into London tomorrow," Susan told the kids as they sat around the table for their evening meal. "We're going to spend the night and come back the next day. Do you guys want to come with us or do you feel comfortable hanging around here?"

"What are ya'll going for?" asked Livi.

Scott took the question. "We're going to meet with a carpenter who specializes in the restoration of timber-framed houses. Hopefully, he can do the work for us. Then we need to shop for supplies and materials. The next morning we're going to meet with Mr. Franklin while we're there. We'll probably be back after lunch."

"I'd rather stay home," said Jack.

"That's fine," said Livi. "I don't mind staying."

"Okay then, you guys hold down the fort," said Susan. "We'll probably leave just after breakfast."

After a pause in the conversation, Jack proffered a question that had been on his mind for a couple of weeks. "Mom, after the house is fixed up, are we really going to sell it?"

"Well, baby, that is the plan. Why do you ask?"

"I kind of like it here," responded Jack. "I wouldn't mind staying."

"You mean live here?" asked Susan.

"You know, I wouldn't mind living here either," chimed in Livi.

Scott turned to Susan and gave her his patented Cheshire grin. "Wait a minute," said Susan. "Have you guys been talking behind my back?"

"I haven't said a word! Promise!" said Scott. In fact, Scott had proposed the same idea to Susan just a few days ago, but had not discussed it with the children.

"Look, I know that this has been fun, but our lives are back home. My work is back home. We can't just pick up and move on a whim," explained Susan. "Remember, we came here to settle the property. Right?"

Jack nodded. "I know, but still."

Susan glanced around the table. "Look, let's just stick to our plan, okay?" she said, less convincingly than she had hoped.

As evening turned into the night, everyone retired to bed. Except for Livi, of course, who dutifully made her way into the upstairs study "just for a few minutes," she told herself. Livi had systematically made her way around the book casings in the room and planned to look through the books on the back wall of the study. She had noted that Hollingsworth had a method in cataloging his tomes: usually by fiction or nonfiction, followed by subject, then book size, and interestingly, by color. Apparently, Lord Jonathan William Augustus Hollingsworth IV was quite compulsive.

So it struck Livi as curious when she scanned the back wall of shelves and one book stood out among the others. It wasn't dramatic, but the color of the binding was just a shade different from the surrounding books. Not only that, the spine of the book was a hair shorter and a fraction wider than that of its neighbors. Again, this finding was nothing dramatic, but just enough to draw Livi's attention. She walked toward the book, which was on the shelf just above her eye level. It was the third book from the end on the right. The title of the book was simply Tempus Est. Livi registered this as another oddity, because Hollingsworth's Latin publications were grouped at the other end of the room. She also noted that no author was referenced upon the spine. Though Livi could not read Latin, her curiosity was piqued and she reached to remove the book from the shelf. She grasped the book and motioned to slide it off the shelf. The book, however, did not budge. Determined, Livi grasped the book at the top of the spine and pulled with greater effort. As she did so, the book pivoted out toward her and she heard a soft "click" like that of a crackling ember of a fire. At the sound, the four-foot section of casing that housed the mysterious book began to retract into the wall. Livi gasped and jumped back, startled as she witnessed the bookshelf recede its entire depth from floor to ceiling, to become askew with the section of casing that remained in place. From behind the casework, a dim light was emitted.

Livi, though tremulous with fear, was more overpowered by curiosity and she stepped toward the shelf. She pressed against the front of the casing in an attempt to push it back further, but to no avail. As she moved closer to inspect it, she noted a space of about three inches to the right of the casing. She slid her hand into the gap and pushed against the side of the bookcase. Feeling some resistance, she began to slide the casing behind the other shelves. When she released pressure, the shelf returned to its original position and locked back into place. Livi presumed the mechanism must be spring-loaded. Once again she grasped the top of the book and pulled it, releasing the lock. This time, Livi opened the casing enough to step into the threshold and block the casing from closing with her body. As she peered in, Livi realized that she had discovered Augustus Hollingsworth's hidden study.

Without thought, Livi stepped into the room. As she crossed the threshold, the shelf began to move back into place. Livi could only stand and watch as the casing latched back into place, leaving her to stare at a bare wall. She turned to take in her surroundings and saw that the dim light she initially noted was coming from the outside. Two small slits in the wall, just under the ceiling, allowed enough moonlight in to silhouette the room. Livi searched the wall for a light switch and, finding none, surmised that this room had not been modernized with electric lights. Instead she found wall sconces with taper boxes nestled below them. She went to each sconce and lit the candles with matches she retrieved from the taper boxes.

With the room a bit more illuminated, Livi was first struck by the sight of an exposed staircase at the back of the room directly across from the secret doorway. With a quick assessment of spatial orientation, Livi concluded that the staircase spiraled down to the library below. She deduced that there must also be a secret chamber behind the back wall of book casings in that room. Next to the staircase against the back wall was another set of book casings, completely adorned with books, manuscripts, notepads and loose papers. These, however, were certainly not in the orderly presentation to which

Livi had become accustomed throughout the rest of the house. In the back corner opposite the staircase was a coat rack upon which hung a heavy sweater, presumably Augustus's.

A large desk cluttered with papers was situated in front of the bookshelves. Behind the desk was a large chair set upon coasters. It appeared to be more utilitarian than comfortable. On the wall adjacent to the side of the desk was a small fireplace. Livi thought that Augustus must have concealed the chimney, as she did not recall seeing such from the outside of the manor. In front of the desk were two small wingback chairs. Other than the sconces, which now illuminated the room, the only other source of light was a single oil-burning lamp upon the desk. She lit that lamp as well, adjusting the wick to the desired brightness, and reflexively stuffed the remaining matches in her pocket. Livi found the room to be quite cozy and fresh despite, she presumed, decades of abandonment. Completely entranced by her discovery, Livi did not consider that she seemingly was trapped within the secret room. She set out to investigate.

As Livi rounded the front of the desk, she briefly scanned its cluttered surface and made her way toward the book casing along the back wall. She noted that the books upon the shelf dealt with physics and calculus, and an assortment of other scientific disciplines. She saw collections of various scientific journals and tablets with handwritten notes and mathematical formulas. Were these Augustus' notes? Livi wondered. She found this collection curious. "Why would Augustus have these books?" she asked aloud. All of the other books in Hollingsworth's vast collection tended toward classic literature, poetry and history. Yet in this room, they were all oriented to the sciences. Except for these... On the lower-most shelf of the book casing she found an interesting collection of novels. Voyage au centre de la Terre (Journey to the Center of the Earth in English, noted Livi) by Jules Verne; The Time Machine, by H.G. Wells; A Yankee at the Court of King Arthur, by Mark Twain ("I thought it was A Connecticut Yankee in King Arthur's Court," pondered Livi). Livi reached down and pulled from the shelf A Yankee at the Court of King Arthur. She opened the front cover and was surprised to find a handwritten note:

Augustus,

Though I find your theories fanciful at best, they have enlightened my mind to the possibilities. I wish you the best of luck with your endeavor. Should anyone achieve such, it would have to be a man of complex intellectual capacity like yourself. In the meanwhile, I trust you will enjoy the fantasy of a simple-minded man. Food for thought.

Sam

1889

"Wow! A note from Mark Twain!" Livi reached for the next book, the French copy of Journey to the Center of the Earth. Again, she opened the cover:

Augie,

I would greatly appreciate any comments you may have regarding this work. I should like to improve upon the scientific accuracy in my future publications. I am in deep appreciation for the hospitality you bestowed upon me as your guest this past fall. I hope to join with you again in discussion of scientific theorem. My best to you always,

Jules

1865

Livi replaced the book and collected the next, H.G. Wells' The Time Machine. With anticipation, she opened the book:

My Dear Friend and Inspiration,

As promised, here is the finished work. As I am sure you will note, my protagonist is based upon you, my mentor. As per your request, I have given no reference, either direct or implied, to you or your research. In fact, my protagonist is not even named. I call him simply, The Time Traveler. To further avoid incrimination, I have had my traveler only adventure to the future, which of course you would never allow. A word of caution: Do not allow your time machine to be discovered lest disastrous effects result. I know the time is near that you will embark upon your adventure. I fear I shall not see you again. My thoughts and prayers are with you.

Herbert
1895

Livi noticed that the date was the year before Augustus' disappearance. "What does that mean?" she voiced aloud. With her heart racing, Livi moved to Augustus' desk. She sat in the large chair and rifled through his papers, feeling somewhat like a trespasser, going as far as to look over her shoulder before proceeding. Beneath a jumbled assortment of loose papers, Livi discovered a tablet containing pages of schematic drawings and accompanying calculations. She noted the first drawing was that of a grandfather clock. Immediately, she recognized it to be the large clock of the library by the indicated measurements and details. Livi continued to peruse the pages. The next few pages contained diagrams of what she concluded to be the inner workings of the timekeeping mechanism. Thinking that she had stumbled upon the explanation for the self-winding clock, she scanned the document closely. "I bet this explains it," she said. But she found nothing that indicated a self-winding mechanism, though she admitted to herself that she might not recognize such. Livi looked further through the papers. Throughout the document, Hollingsworth had made sketches and notations.

"Neither Galilean nor Newtonian theories of relativity apply to time/spatial arrangements."

Within the body of the text were algorithms of calculus formulations, which Livi did not recognize but could interpret. She read further.

"Hemholtz's postulations have merit. I must determine how they apply to sub-mass disruption. More work is required in determining the smallest component of a man."

For hours Livi read such similar computations, notations, and references to the greatest scientist of the day, noting that "the day" was the nineteenth century. The night had waned into the early morning hours when she reached the ending pages of Hollingsworth's bound notes. It was in the reading of these last few pages, replete with calculations, notations and diagrams, that the meaning of the document was elucidated.

"No way! It can't be." Livi look more intently at the diagrams. Though her mind was having trouble processing at the early hour, as it was now close to 7:30 a.m., the conclusion was foregone. Within the clock, Hollingsworth had drawn a chamber, a room so to speak. But the mathematical calculations suggested that this was actually a virtual room. "He created virtual reality before computers were invented!" If her interpretations were correct, when one entered the grandfather clock of the library, one entered the portal of a--

"This is crazy, it's impossible!" Despite her attempts to convince herself otherwise, Livi had discovered that Augustus Hollingsworth had created a time machine. "I've got to find Jack. I have to tell Mom and Dad!"

With her conclusions firmly seated within her brain, Livi set off to reveal the discovery to her family. It was at this point that she realized that she knew not how to extricate herself from the secret study. She turned toward the staircase. "Well, that must go somewhere."

Livi descended the spiral staircase to the first floor. She noted the same type of slits in the wall adjacent to the ceiling, but this time, the morning sunlight was coming through. It was only then that Livi realized she had been up all night.

The room into which the stairs descended was not much larger than a storage closet. Mounted upon the wall was a single sconce, which Livi lit with a match from her pocket. With nothing to distract her, Livi quickly noted a track running parallel with the wall that abutted the library, and a pedal protruding from the base of this wall. She surmised that this pedal would activate a hidden door that led into the library, and resolved to ascertain if a similar mechanism existed in Hollingsworth's secret study. Livi depressed the pedal with her foot. With that act, a small section of the wall retracted toward Livi. She then pushed the section along its track, causing it to slide behind the remaining segment of wall, thus exposing the library. As Livi stepped into the library, the section of book casing returned to its original location, hiding any evidence of the passage through which Livi had just emerged. When she inspected this casing from the library side, Livi noted the same book that had activated the secret door of the upstairs study.

Livi walked through the library until she was directly in front of the large grandfather clock. She looked at it intently, even pressing her face against the opaque glass of the door in a futile attempt to peer inside. She stepped back, incredulous at the idea that this was Hollingsworth's time machine.

Livi set upon her mission to notify her family of the discovery. She walked to the double doors that led into the evening parlor and opened them. As she stepped through the doorway, she noted an unfamiliar voice coming from the breakfast room. The voice was that of a male, but the accent was strange. The man was speaking an English dialect that Livi had never before heard. She eased herself across the entryway and into the morning parlor. As she did so, she heard her father speak.

"What are your intentions for the house in the event that we sell it to you?" Scott asked.

"Sir, it is the intention of your most humble servant to reside here," answered the strange voice. Hearing this, Livi stopped in her tracks and maneuvered herself further away from the doorway to avoid being seen. "Oh no," she whispered to herself softly.

"I'm afraid that this is all rather sudden," said Scott. "And really, it would be best for you to speak with our attorney. He is the person that is dealing with the sale of the property."

Livi heard the sound of a chair sliding back. "I'll get you his card. Now, I will be happy to show you out." Livi heard the sound of a second chair sliding back.

"Mr. Hawthorne, time is of the imperative, I fear," responded the voice. "I am prepared to settle with sterling silver in the amount that you stipulate." The man continued, "My associate and I have only the best intentions for this magnificent property. Shall we have an accord, sir?"

Suddenly, Livi saw the owner of the voice step forward with his hand extended. He was dressed in what appeared to be a costume consisting of a Puritan tunic and cloak. In his other hand he held a hat. Another man, of ragged appearance, stepped up behind the Puritan. As this man moved into Livi's line of sight, he made eye contact with her. He appeared startled when he saw her and paused to stare, as though he recognized her. The man who had been speaking then looked at Livi, to discover his assistant's distraction. As he glared at Livi, he pulled the ragged man forward and the two of them moved out of Livi's line of sight.

Susan, hidden from Livi's view as was Scott, spoke next. "I'm sorry, but we were just headed out to an appointment and we really must be going. You'll have to discuss your proposal with our attorney," she said.

The Puritan was not to be put off. "Madam, we shall return tomorrow with a case of sterling and the hope of finalizing a transaction. Perhaps your representative can join us then. I should like to execute this arrangement promptly. Shall we see you this time on the morrow?" asked the man.

"I'm afraid that we won't be available until tomorrow evening," Susan informed him.

"Tomorrow eve, then. Now, we shall take our leave," said the man.

Livi, not wishing to see this "creepy" man again, quietly and quickly made her way upstairs.

# CHAPTER 6

# Jack and Livi Devise a Plan

As Livi bounded onto the upper landing, she had all but forgotten the fatigue resulting from her sleepless night. The adrenaline coursing through her veins had revitalized her. She turned right and made her way into Jack's room, where he lay sleeping in peaceful ignorance of what Livi had in store. She closed the door quietly behind her and urgently whispered, "Jack! Wake up!"

Not unexpectedly, Jack did not stir. The once early riser had only recently morphed into the stereotypical adolescent bed-slug. Livi moved toward Jack and none too gently rustled him awake. "Jack, get up!"

Jack cracked one eye open and regarded his sister. "What?"

"Mom and Dad are going to sell the house," she said.

Still trying to come to grips with consciousness, Jack propped himself up on his elbows. "When? To whom?" he asked.

"To some creepy guy, maybe tomorrow," replied Livi.

Jack was still somewhat disoriented. "Tomorrow?"

Livi lowered herself to the edge of Jack's bed and sat. "We can't let that happen, Jack. I've found something that you aren't going to believe."

"What?" lazily queried Jack.

Livi, knowing that what she was about to say would sound implausible, responded with some degree of hesitancy. "You know the grandfather clock in the library?"

"Yeah," acknowledged Jack.

"I think it's a time machine."

Jack, not quite sure if Livi was being serious, eyed her skeptically. "A time machine?"

"A time travel machine," clarified Livi.

Jack looked at his sister intently for a moment as the comment sank into his being. "Right," he said as he lay back down and pulled the covers over his head.

At that moment, there was a light knock upon the door as Susan opened it. "Oh, there you are. What are you doing in here?" she addressed Livi. "Why are you still in those clothes?" she asked, noting that Livi was still wearing the clothing she'd had on the day before.

With a barely perceptible stammer, Livi answered, "I fell asleep reading. I'm trying to get Jack up to help me in the study."

"That's not--" Jack's statement was interrupted by a subtle, yet effective punch in the kidney.

"Oh, okay," said Susan suspiciously. "Well, we're heading off for London. We'll be back tomorrow, sometime in the afternoon," Susan reported.

"Okay, Mom, we'll be fine," said Livi earnestly.

Susan, just a bit curious, made to leave. "Well, call if you need anything. And lock the doors when the workers leave."

"Okay, have a good trip," said Livi.

"Bye, Mom," said a muffled Jack from underneath the covers.

Susan eased out of the room, eyeing her children as she closed the door behind her. Livi waited for a moment, and then ripped the covers off of Jack. "I'm not kidding, Jack!" she insisted.

Jack again cracked one eye open, the look itself conveying the doubt that he felt.

"Come on, I'll show you," said Livi.

"Show me what, the clock? I've seen it," replied Jack.

"No." Livi paused. "Hollingsworth's secret study."

Jack sat up in bed and looked Livi in the eye. "Secret study?" After a moment, he came to a conclusion. "I gotta pee." With that, he got up and went into the bathroom adjoining his room.

Livi spoke through the door that Jack had closed behind him. "Last night I found Hollingsworth's hidden study. He drew plans for a time machine. He has calculations and diagrams and theorems and postulates." She paused for a moment as she heard the flush of the toilet. "I think that the grandfather clock in the library is his time machine. Jack, the science makes sense. I think it really works."

Jack turned off the tap, opened the door and stepped into his room. As he regarded his sister, he said, "Show me." "Hold on," Livi said as she moved toward the window that overlooked the front drive. As she peered out the window, she saw Scott and Susan get into the car and drive off. "Okay, let's go."

Livi quickly moved toward the bedroom door and opened it. Jack followed behind sluggishly. The two crossed the upper landing and entered the upstairs study. By the time Jack entered the room, Livi was at the back casing and had her hand on the book that triggered the passage into Hollingsworth's hidden study. "Ready?" Livi asked, making sure that she had Jack's attention. Jack shrugged an unenthusiastic, sleepy assent. Livi pivoted the book forward, once again setting the case into motion.

In an instant, Jack was awake. His mouth gaped open in wonderment and his eyes widened in amazement. "You're not kidding," was all he could mutter. The siblings entered the study and, as before, the case moved back into place. "Come see," directed Livi as she moved behind Hollingsworth's desk. As he moved to join Livi, Jack peered around the small room. "Whoa, this is amazing!"

"Look!" said Livi, indicating Hollingsworth's papers as Jack sidled up beside her.

Livi and Jack pored over Hollingsworth's documents for hours. Livi explained the science as best she could interpret it and Jack, to his own astonishment, found that it did indeed make sense. They looked over letters of correspondence written back and forth between Hollingsworth and leading scientists of his day. Such men as Heinrich Hertz, James Maxwell and Willard Gibbs had weighed in on Hollingsworth's theories of time travel.

"Haven't you stayed in the library at night to see how the clock wound itself?" Livi asked Jack.

"Yeah, a couple of times," he replied.

"Well, what did you see?" followed Livi.

"Nothing," admitted Jack. After a pause, "I fell asleep both times."

"Fell asleep?" asked Livi, incredulous at Jack's admission.

"I couldn't help it! I got bored," said Jack in his defense.

After a few more moments of looking through Hollingsworth's documents, Livi uttered her conclusion. "We have to get into that clock. We have to find out if the clock is Hollingsworth's time machine before Mom and Dad sell the house."

Jack thought a moment. "Well, let's tell Mom and Dad when they get home. We'll show them all of this stuff. Mom can figure it out."

Livi pondered for a moment. "No, we have to find out if it works before Mom and Dad get back. That man is coming back tomorrow to buy the house. If we wait until they get home, it may be too late."

"Okay then. Let's do it," Jack said enthusiastically as he began to move. Then, a bit uncertainly, he asked, "How do we get out of here?"

"We can't work on it now. There's going to be too many workers coming in and out. We have to wait until they're gone for the day. Anyway, I'm exhausted. I need some rest, I was up all night," said Livi.

"Well, while you're sleeping, I'll look through everything in here and see if I can find out how to get into the clock. If I can't find anything, I'll try to figure something out," said Jack. "I'll wake you up around five. By then, all of the workers will be gone and we can get started."

"Okay," said Livi as she rose and walked toward the closed passage. She depressed the pedal that opened the passage back into the study. "This is how you get out. Don't let anyone find you in here." With that, Livi stepped into the study. As the case moved back into place, she quickly uttered a warning: "And don't break anything. Especially the clock."

Jack did indeed look over the entire study, inch by inch. He found diagrams of the clock door with reference to an intricate locking mechanism. Apparently, the key to the door operated on some electromagnetic principle that allowed the tumbler mechanism to be released and align with the key. He looked feverishly for the referenced key, but to no avail. Jack even took the staircase down to the small anteroom behind the library to look for any clues, but came away empty handed.

He ultimately eased his way into the library to steal a closer look at the clock and its impenetrable door. As craftsmen meandered in and out, completing the finish work in the library, Jack made small talk and pretended to read, all the while studying the clock with deep intent. After a small bite for sustenance, Jack traipsed into his parents' room to avail himself of the Internet connection that they enjoyed in their master suite. He easily hacked past the parental controls and researched all he could find with regard to grandfather clocks, electromagnetism and locks, learning more than he ever knew existed on the topics.

As five o'clock neared and the last of the craftsmen left for the day, Jack concluded that he had no idea how to get into the clock. In just a few minutes, he would wake Livi and give her the bad news.

After fielding a phone call from Scott and Susan and assuring them that all was well, Jack and Livi sat down to a dinner of frozen pizza and juice. Neither was hungry, but felt they would need energy for what promised to be a long night.

"We'll have to pick the lock," said Livi between bites. "But how?" she added.

"I've been thinking about that," said Jack with a mouthful of pepperoni and cheese, which Livi noted with disgust.

"Please swallow before you talk, that is so gross. I hope you don't ever go on a dinner date."

Jack managed to swallow with the assistance of a gulp of juice. "I've been thinking about that," he said again. "We need to generate an electromagnetic field. We can get a battery and attach the leads to a wire coiled around a metal pin, and try to pick the lock that way."

"Can you do that?" asked Livi.

"Yeah, we have everything we need with all of the construction material around," Jack replied.

"Well, it's our only chance. But if we break the lock, we'll never know if the clock really is a time machine," said Livi.

"Are you sure that the electromagnetic lock is tied in to the virtual portal?" asked Jack.

"The way Hollingsworth's papers read, if the electromagnetic field is disrupted, the time portal is lost. It's a safety feature to prevent anyone from tampering with the time machine. So, as long as the lock is not disrupted and the clock continues to run, the time machine will work. At least theoretically."

"Great. No pressure," said Jack sarcastically.

Jack and Livi cleared away their dishes and set off to work. Jack gathered the supplies that he needed to generate an electromagnetic field. He collected batteries of various voltage as well as differing-gauge electrical wire. Livi collected the diagrams that Hollingsworth had left behind in his study. The pair assembled all that they had in the library and set to work by the glow of a single lamp. They spent hours trying to find the correct combination of batteries and wires to generate the electromagnetic field that Hollingsworth had specified in his papers.

As the hour approached midnight, they fell upon the precise formula. Now came the time to put their work to the test. With the electromagnetic field generated, Jack extended the metal pin through the coil and into the lock mechanism. He began to work delicately and steadily. Livi noted with some admiration that Jack never wavered in concentration, even as she began to lose hope.

And then it happened. It was so subtle that neither Jack nor Livi was sure that it really had. "Did you hear that?" Jack asked. "Yes," affirmed Livi.

What they heard was the slightest "whirr" followed by a barely perceptible click. Jack advanced the improvised key farther. A second click was emitted. After another few millimeters of advancement a third click was heard and the lock released, causing the door to the grandfather clock to crack slightly ajar. At that very moment, the chimes of the clock began to strike the midnight hour. The sound, quite loud with the door ajar, startled the children and caused them both to jump back, Jack toppling onto his backside. They stared for a moment at the clock, mesmerized by its tone. Then they looked at each other, surprised that they had actually mastered the lock.

It was then that it hit them both. They had opened the clock. Now what were they going to do? Before they could answer the question, even before they could voice it to each other, they heard another familiar sound. As the resonance of the chimes began to fade, they heard what was unmistakably whistling. Jack turned to look at the library doors in quick succession, trying to determine where the sound originated. He turned his gaze to Livi, whose eyes were wide with fright. It then occurred to him that the whistling was coming from inside the clock.

# CHAPTER 7

# Jack and Livi Meet Augustus

In an instant, Jack and Livi darted behind an oversized leather chair to take cover, each peering around opposite sides at the clock. The whistling became louder. Then the two heard chains clattering in a rhythmic pattern, which they knew to be the sound of someone winding the clock. It was as the third weight was raised, completing the process, that the whistling abruptly stopped. Jack motioned to Livi, indicating the door to exit the library. Livi nodded in assent. As they were preparing to bolt, they were stopped dead in their tracks by the sight of a hand reaching around the edge of the clock door from inside. Jack and Livi ducked back behind the chair once more, burying their faces into its back.

Joshua Kingsley had no idea that this day would be different than any other. Why would it? Time in the clock stood still, especially when one had control of it. Days went by like seconds, years like minutes. So, as he set about his task of winding the clock for the week, he had no reason to be especially attentive. He had just returned from a very enjoyable journey, and took the opportunity to relive the memory in the moments of solitude that he would have until Augustus returned.

As he pulled the last weight of the clock mechanism to its apogee, he noticed an unfamiliar glow reflecting off the pendulum. He negotiated his way past the swinging object and stood beneath the weights. He saw that the clock door was ajar and light from the library was seeping in. His heart began to race. He looked back to see if there was any sign of Augustus, but he had not yet returned. Should he wait? No, he couldn't; he was too excited. Anyway, it would be better for him to go out. Though older than Augustus, he was stronger. The effects would not be as impactful on him.

Kingsley reached around the door and slowly pushed it open. He saw papers and wires strewn about the floor in front of him. He stepped out of the clock and immediately felt the process begin. He knew he didn't have much time. Kingsley glanced around the room. He was about to call out when he saw them.

A mirror on the back wall revealed the reflection of two children crouched behind a chair, faces buried into its back. Kingsley smiled and began to whistle again. He turned his back to the children, presuming that they would eventually peek around the chair to spy on him.

He moved slowly and deliberately. He saw the improvised key protruding from the keyhole of the door and removed it, letting it fall to the floor. He admired the ingenuity. Then, with exaggerated movements, he took a large key from his coat pocket, raising it higher than necessary to inspect it. He slowly turned, noting the children ducking back behind the chair. As he watched them in the mirror (to which they were oblivious), he eased over to the single lamp that illuminated the room, whistling all the while, and turned it off. He returned to the clock and, when he reached it, stopped whistling. Kingsley closed the clock door and locked it.

Jack and Livi, after seeing the hand protruding from the clock, hid quietly. When the whistling resumed, they each chanced a look at its origin. What they saw was the figure of a tall black man who appeared to be in his late thirties, wearing what appeared to be an old-style suit of clothes. They saw the man remove the key that they had fashioned from the lock of the clock door and drop it to the floor. He then reached into his coat pocket and produced a large, ornate key that he brought up to the level of his eyes. The key was gold, and the bow of the key was studded with what appeared to be sparkling diamonds that surrounded a crest. As the man began to slowly turn, Jack and Livi ducked once again behind the chair. They heard his movement behind the whistling; then they were immersed into total darkness with the click of the switch of the single lamp that had provided light to the library. Though they could not see, they heard the man return to the clock. As the door closed, the whistling stopped.

Upon hearing the familiar whirr and subsequent tumbling of the lock mechanism, they knew that their effort to gain entry into the clock had been thwarted. Though neither said it aloud, they were both relieved. The children remained behind the chair, not moving a muscle, their breathing barely audible. After a few moments of silence, they looked at each other and nodded in mutual agreement that the man had returned to the clock, and all was clear.

Jack was the first to slowly rise from behind the chair. Livi followed suit. The children made their way around their respective sides of the chair and headed toward the clock. Jack felt his way to the lamp and switched it back on. Light filled the room, as did the sound of Livi's piercing scream.

Livi was facing the clock as the light came on. As it did so, she saw in the door of the clock the reflection of the tall black man. She whipped around to gaze upon his menacing face, simultaneously emitting a scream. It took a moment for Jack to realize what was happening. When he did, he too let out a scream (a bit too shrill, as he would later recall). Joshua Kingsley had not reentered the clock. Instead, he'd crept around the periphery of the library, coming to rest directly behind the children. Kingsley now advanced toward the children, who in turn moved closer to each other, cowering in fear. At the moment that Kingsley reached the children, towering above them, his ominous demeanor gently morphed into a kindly expression. In a booming baritone voice replete with a proper British accent, Joshua addressed the children: "Hello there. And what are your names?"

Still shaken, Livi replied, "Please don't hurt us."

Jack also lobbied, "Yeah, we didn't mean anything, really."

"Hurt you? Oh my, I have no intention of any such thing," said Kingsley, incredulous at the thought. "I am Joshua Kingsley. I am the caretaker here." With a bow, he added, "At your service." When he straightened, he asked the children, "Again, who might you be?"

Jack, still taken aback but feeling a bit more at ease, responded first. "I'm Jack Hawthorne. This is my sister, Olivia."

Joshua acknowledged Jack with a bow. "Master Jack." And with the same genteel gesture he acknowledged Livi. "Mistress Olivia."

"My friends call me Livi," she explained, still somewhat tremulous.

"Mistress Livi then, for I should like to count myself a friend," replied Kingsley. With an exaggerated gesture of open arms, Kingsley then said, "Welcome to Hollingsworth Manor. We have been expecting you." Jack and Livi looked at each other, curious as to the meaning of Kingsley's remark.

"Now, judging by the appearance of your efforts, I presume you wish to enter the clock," Kingsley stated.

"Can we?" asked Jack hopefully.

"But of course," said Kingsley. "After all, that is why you are here, true?"

"Mr. Kingsley, is the clock a time travel machine?" Livi queried.

Kingsley regarded her intently. Momentarily, a large smile appeared upon his face as he replied, "Indeed it is, Mistress Livi. Indeed it is." He once again removed the large key from his pocket and moved toward the clock. He placed the key into the lock and opened the door. With a sweeping motion of his long arm, he gestured into the clock. "Shall we?" In an instant, Jack, Livi and Kingsley were inside.

Kingsley led the way through the clock mechanism, cautioning the children to avoid the pendulum as they traversed its arching path. As the trio advanced past the pendulum, Jack and Livi noticed a strange sensation. With each forward step they took, they seemed to accelerate in reverse. Blurred images seemed to be passing them by at tremendous speed. The effect was somewhat nauseating. The sound of the clock's ticking quickly receded as their surroundings whirred past them in a blur. Just as suddenly as this sensation of reverse acceleration had come upon them, all sense of motion ceased and the three found themselves in the library that they had just left, standing with their backs to the large grandfather clock.

But was this the same library, Livi wondered? Though it appeared to be, it was somewhat different. The furnishings were pristine and the books on the shelves appeared newly bound. The room was perfectly lit though no lights appeared to be on, and its climate was perfectly comfortable. Another oddity was that the surroundings shimmered intermittently.

Jack, too, felt something to be different and he was perplexed. "Where are we?" asked Jack.

"Why, Master Jack, we are in the clock, of course," answered Kingsley.

"It looks like we're back in the library," Jack said.

"Indeed it does," acknowledged Kingsley.

"Is this real?" asked Livi, considering the possibility.

"It is as real as you perceive, Mistress Livi," Kingsley said.

The reality, or rather the lack thereof, struck Livi. "This is Hollingsworth's virtual antechamber! Oh my gosh! He actually created a virtual reality!"

"Well, I don't know about virtual reality, but this is indeed the vestibule to the time portal," Kingsley said. "You have obviously studied Augustus' designs," he added.

"So we're not really in the library? We're imagining all of this?" Jack asked with confusion.

"Master Jack, who is to say what is real? Isn't it true that if you experience something, if you perceive it, then it is indeed real?" Kingsley posed.

"I don't know what's real anymore. This is all weird," Jack determined.

"Master Jack, do you have dreams?" Kingsley asked.

"Sure I do," Jack said.

"I submit to you that those dreams are real. They're real in a different realm of existence, a different reality, but real nonetheless. Existence in this clock, this time portal is just as real. We are just in a different plane of existence," Kingsley explained.

Jack looked at Kingsley with suspicion. "I have no idea what you're talking about."

Kingsley laughed. "Fear not, Master Jack, you will come to understand in good time."

As Jack and Kingsley engaged in their surreal conversation, Livi took the opportunity to explore this virtual world. Everything she encountered in the room had a quality of realism, but was somehow artificial. As she sank her hand into a cushion, it took an instant before it molded to her hand. She pulled a book from the shelf and noted that words appeared on the pages only as she turned them. The flames of the burning tapers did not burn and the fireplace, though crackling with glowing embers, emitted no heat. The windows had no view, revealing only diffuse light.

Livi's exploration was interrupted by the sound of a different vibrant British voice, growing in intensity. "Joshua, do you have my hat? I'm afraid I have once again left it behind. I really must be more careful." As the voice grew louder the three turned toward the clock, from which the voice was coming. "What a marvelous adventure, didn't you think so, Joshua?"

With this question, the clock's shape transformed into a shimmering mist as Augustus Hollingsworth, a virile young man in his early thirties, emerged from the vapor and entered the room, dressed as though he had just been on a fox hunt. As he spied Kingsley, he asked again, "So, Joshua, did you retrieve my hat?"

"I'm afraid not, Augustus," Kingsley replied.

"Well, ballyhoo. Oh well, surely I can procure another," Augustus chortled. As he advanced, Augustus took note of Jack. "Here, boy, take care of this." Augustus dropped the riding cape he had slung over his shoulder into Jack's hands as he walked past him. "Wasn't that a lovely adventure, Joshua? Did you see...?"

At that moment, Augustus stopped dead in his tracks, suddenly realizing that a stranger was within the vestibule. He slowly turned to regard the boy he had entrusted with his cape. He noted another person from the corner of his eye and turned a bit more to see a young lady standing by the bookcases, staring at him with her mouth agape.

Kingsley broke the silence. "Lord Hollingsworth, may I present Mistress Livi and Master Jack Hawthorne. They are siblings." Then, addressing the children, he said, "Children, may I introduce Lord Jonathan William Augustus Hollingsworth IV."

As Livi made her way over, Jack extended a hand. "Nice to meet you, sir." Augustus absently took his hand and shook it. Livi extended her hand likewise. "It's a pleasure to meet you, Lord Hollingsworth." Augustus released Jack's hand, took Livi's and with some small degree of his composure restored, returned the salutation, bowing as he did so. "The pleasure is mine, Mistress." Augustus straightened as he released Livi's hand and turned inquiringly to Kingsley. Kingsley met his inquisitive gaze with his trademark broad grin. "Mistress Livi and Master Jack opened the door."

Augustus began to feel faint. He maneuvered himself to the nearest settee and sank into its cushion, his eyes locked on Kingsley. "They opened the door?" Augustus asked, making certain that he had heard correctly.

"They did indeed," Kingsley assured him.

Augustus then addressed the children, "You opened the door to the clock?"

Jack, now thinking that their plan to invade the clock was not such a good one, mounted a defense. "We just wanted to see it. We didn't think we would cause any trouble."

Livi then interjected, "It's my fault, sir. I found your design for the time portal. I talked Jack into helping me."

Augustus regarded the children for a moment, and then bolted to a standing position. With laughing excitement, he exclaimed, "You opened the door! You two marvelous children opened the door! Oh how we have been waiting for you!" And with that, Augustus gathered the children into a warm, welcoming embrace, laughing all the while.

"Now children, come and tell me all about your discovery." He led Jack and Livi to an arrangement of chairs and bade them sit down. Kingsley, with his patented grin and a tear of joy trailing down his cheek, addressed the group. "I shall gather refreshments." Augustus exhorted, "Yes, Joshua, do. And hurry back, I don't want you to miss a single detail."

Augustus, Kingsley, Livi and Jack talked for what seemed an eternity. Livi and Jack told Augustus how they came to be in Colchester. They traced through the family tree and determined the exact relationship that the children had to Augustus.

Livi and Jack told the two men how they discovered Augustus' secret study and devised a key to enter the clock. Augustus marveled at their deductive powers and ingenuity. He interrupted frequently to urge even greater detail as he reveled in their story. They told Augustus of the legend of the self-winding clock, and how Hollingsworth Manor was reputed to be haunted in light of the mysterious disappearance of Augustus and Kingsley in 1896. Kingsley laughed at the thought of himself being considered a ghost.

Augustus, in turn, detailed to the children how he became fascinated with time travel. He told of the apprenticeship that his father arranged with the Colchester clockmaker, Samuel Downum, who was himself apprenticed by Colchester's most famous clockmaker, John Smorthwaite. Augustus told how he made the clocks of all types that littered the manor, and explained how he became a member of The Worshipful Company of Clockmakers. He revealed that it was through that membership, and his social station as Lord of Hollingsworth Manor, that he gained access to the greatest literary and scientific minds of his time. Augustus described the many conversations and correspondences with these great minds by which he developed his theorems for time travel. The relationships he forged fostered his desire and ability to create this time travel machine.

Jack and Livi listened attentively. The tale was fascinating on many levels. When all was said and done, Jack posed a question: "How does the time machine work?"

Augustus broke into a smile, looking back and forth from Jack to Livi. "I'm not going to tell you, Jack. I'm going to show you. When in time do you want to go?"

# CHAPTER 8

# The Time Machine

Jack and Livi looked at one another, shocked by the realization that they were actually going to travel in time. Neither said a word. Augustus, confusing their hesitation for lack of interest, addressed them again. "Surely you two have something in the past you would like to see."

Jack spoke up, "Of course we do! Can we go anywhere, anytime?"

Augustus gleefully replied, "Indeed you can. Well, anytime. Anywhere is a bit more complex. You see, when we exit the time portal, we will be in the physical location of this house. If we wish to travel away from Colchester, we will have to do so by means available at the time."

Livi then posed the next question. "Can we travel to the future?"

Augustus became very serious and stern. "Children, you may never, ever travel to the future."

Taken aback by Augustus' sudden change of demeanor, Jack probed further, "Why not?"

Augustus explained, "The future is not for us to see. If one were to see the future, it would affect one's actions during their lifetime. Time travel poses risks. Any action one takes in a time other than one's own may affect the course of history. In the past, we know the history and we can protect it from alteration. We cannot safeguard the future in the same way. It is much too dangerous. In any event, if my theories are correct, if one were to travel to a time past the point of their natural life, their body would begin a process of accelerated aging. One could only survive in the future for a few weeks."

Augustus suddenly jumped to his feet, his carefree persona back in place. "So, what shall it be? Livi, you choose first, won't you? When would you like to see?"

Livi considered for a moment, then said, "Well, I would like to see Charles Dickens. I discovered that he was a reporter in Colchester in the 1830s."

Augustus considered for a moment. "Dickens. Hmm, that name does sound familiar. Ahh, I remember. He wrote Pickwick I do believe. That is such a charming comedy."

Livi added, "He also wrote Oliver Twist."

Augustus again thought for a moment. "I don't recall that one. No matter, let's see if we can find him."

Livi and Augustus went through the library's manuscripts and found that Dickens indeed was in Colchester in 1835, reporting on Parliamentary matters for The

Evening Chronicle. Augustus was in a state of excitement that Kingsley had not seen in some time. Kingsley noted that Jack, on the other hand, seemed a bit blasé as Augustus and Livi pored over tomes relating to 1835 Colchester. He motioned Jack over and suggested an exploration of the workings of the time machine.

Kingsley led Jack toward the large grandfather clock. Off to its side, previously unrecognized by Jack, was what appeared to be a smaller scale model of the timepiece. This version stood about a foot taller than Jack. Kingsley opened the glass door that protected the face of that clock and began to give instruction.

"This is how we set the time to which we plan to travel." Kingsley indicated a dial at the top that tracked the phases of the moon. Beneath this dial were numbers, which Jack took to signify days of the month. Kingsley proceeded to roll the moon dial, saying as he did so, "We align the moon with the day of the month to which we want to travel."

Jack noted with curiosity that Kingsley moved the dial to the number zero. "See here now." Kingsley indicated four rows of numbers, zero to nine, each with an accompanying slide lever. "Each lever is set to the number corresponding to the year of desired travel, Anno Domini."

"Anno Domini?" questioned Jack.

"Yes, Master Jack. The year of our Lord," answered Kingsley.

"Oh! A.D.," said Jack with realization. He then added, "Where's B.C.?"

"We cannot travel that far back, Master Jack. We can only go back as far in time as this house, in some form, existed. The portal is irrevocably linked to the manor," Kingsley explained.

"So how far back can you go?" Jack persisted.

"The earliest existence of this house was as a garrison for a legion of Roman soldiers under the command of Claudius, Emperor of Rome. It was built in 43 A.D."

"Wow," was all that Jack could manage.

Kingsley set all of the levers to zero. He then indicated the face of the clock, which contained the hands and a dial that alternated the image of the sun and the moon, depending upon whether it was day or night. This dial was an exact duplicate of the dial of the original clock in the library.

"This sets the time of day at which we are to arrive in the past." Kingsley set the hands to indicate midnight, then swept his hand in a motion that presented the final result. "This setting brings us to present time. We always return one minute later than the time we left." He then stepped back and indicated the large grandfather clock. "Shall we?"

Jack turned, and was startled by Livi and Augustus. They were behind him, apparently having been there for some time. Livi had retrieved a remote fact of trivia as it bolted from the temporal region of her brain to her consciousness. "Wait a second," she exclaimed. "Calendars have changed. How did you get accurate dates for time travel, Lord Hollingsworth?"

"Very good, Olivia! Very good indeed! How right you are," Augustus said. "Oh, what a challenge it was to synchronize all of those calendars, nearly impossible." Augustus took a short reflective pause. "Actually, since we can only travel back to 43 A.D., I only had to account for three calendars. Still, it was challenging. First, I had to reconcile the Roman calendars, the Julian calendar to be precise, with the Dionysian Calendar. That, in turn, had to be reconciled with the Gregorian calendar, which I'm sure you know became the official calendar of Britain in 1751."

Augustus took another reflective pause. "Oh, and then I neglected to make distinction between common years and leap years. You remember that near disaster, don't you, Joshua? I had to recalculate everything. You see, Olivia, every year that is exactly divisible by 4 is a leap year, except for years that are exactly divisible by 100; these centurial years are leap years only if they are exactly divisible by 400. Well, you can see that if I had neglected that, there is no telling when in history we would have ended up. In any event, all of those variables are incorporated into the time selector. So there you have it."

Olivia and Jack stared dumbfounded at Augustus. Kingsley issued his kindly smile. Augustus, satisfied that all were duly impressed with his exhortations, addressed Kingsley. "Joshua, perhaps you should lead the way." Kingsley responded with a small bow, then walked into the clock, which transformed to a glimmering refraction of light as he did so. Augustus indicated to Livi and Jack to follow, and Augustus followed behind them.

Once again, Jack and Livi experienced the strange sensation that they were moving at an accelerated pace, though their actual stride had not quickened. This time, however, they appeared to be moving forward, passing blurred images as though racing by them. And just as before, all motion suddenly stopped and the group of four found themselves underneath the massive weights within the mechanism of the clock. The pendulum, which was just in front of them, swung lazily, emitting a loud tick-tock as it reached its opposite apogees. The glass door of the clock was just past the pendulum, allowing the travelers to peer into the darkened library of Hollingsworth Manor.

"Where are we now?" asked Jack.

"We are where we have been along all along. Inside the clock," answered Augustus.

"Are we in the present?" queried Livi.

"Indeed we are, Olivia," Augustus replied.

"But why come to the present?" Livi continued. "Our present is your future, isn't it? You can't live in the future, you said so yourself."

"Ah, not quite, Olivia. I told you that we could not survive for more than a few weeks in the future."

"Then why do you come?" Livi persisted.

Augustus looked at Livi as though the answer was obvious. "Well, to wind the clock, of course," Kingsley chimed in. "Mistress Olivia, the clock must continue running for the time portal to remain open. If the clock were to stop, we would be trapped in whatever time we happened to be. Every week at the stroke of midnight, I travel to the present to wind the clock. Neither Augustus nor myself has ever emerged from the clock in what is our future until today."

"Because we had opened the door?" asked Jack.

"Precisely, Jack!" exclaimed Augustus. "Because you opened the door. You and Olivia solved the puzzle and earned entrance into the clock."

Livi considered further. "You said that we have been in the clock the whole time."

"Indeed we have," answered Augustus, curious to see if Livi could further decipher its mysteries.

"So, the room we were just in is not really the library."

"Go on," Augustus encouraged.

"It's a virtual room," Livi proposed.

Augustus, not familiar with the term, looked at Livi for clarification. Livi continued, "It's not what it appears. It's not real." A beaming smile of acknowledgement formed upon Augustus' face. "Very good, Olivia. Very good indeed."

Augustus, Kingsley, Livi and Jack spent considerable time in the vestibule of the time portal. Kingsley showed Jack and Livi how the clock was wound and how the mechanism functioned. Augustus explained the science behind the machine and how he devised its intricacies. The four then traveled back through the portal to the virtual library. There, Augustus related to Jack and

Livi how he and Kingsley first entered the clock in 1896, and how they had chosen the year 1854 to be their base time of operation. It was in this year that the four were now sitting in the virtual room conversing. Augustus explained to an ever-questioning Livi how it was he created and maintained the virtual library. He showed her diagrams, schematics and mathematical equations. Livi not only understood, but also marveled at the utter simplicity of the physical science that Augustus had employed. Jack listened intently and absorbed what he could. He thought surely he could somehow incorporate these phenomena into his magic act.

Their conversation continued. Augustus related the story of his youth. He told how, after he was apprenticed to the local clockmaker, he had come to be married, of the death of his wife at a young age, having borne no children. Kingsley told the children of his relationship to Augustus. Kingsley was an enslaved servant at the Hollingsworth estate. Though Augustus was a couple of years younger, he had befriended Kingsley, and Augustus' parents were instrumental in securing the Emancipation Act of the British Empire in 1833. Kingsley explained that when Augustus became head of the estate upon his parents' deaths, he granted those servants who stayed on, as waged employees, plots of land to have as their own.

As the hours of conversation and discovery waned, Augustus made to prepare for a visit to 1835. While he provided instruction for the impending journey, Kingsley departed to procure appropriate clothing for Jack and Livi. Augustus felt it would be "quite distracting if the children were to emerge into 1835 Colchester in the textiles they purport to be modern clothing." Precisely one minute later, Kingsley once again entered the virtual library through the clock, this time carrying a stack of wrapped and bound parcels.

"Ah ha, very good, Joshua. Let's see what you have there," Augustus exclaimed as he jumped up, excited as a child on Christmas morning.

Kingsley set the paper-wrapped bundles down upon the table and separated them into two piles. "These are for Mistress Olivia," he said as he indicated the pile to his right. "And these are for Master Jack," indicating the other bundle.

Livi and Jack stood motionless. Augustus looked at them perplexed. "Well, have at it, children. Tear into them. Let's see what you have gotten." Jack and Livi looked at each other, then moved toward their respective bundles and began to unwrap.

Livi, who had infinitely more parcels than Jack, found a pair of black leather, ankle-high lace-up shoes, silk stockings, an assortment of undergarments, most of which she could not identify, a blue mutton-sleeved cotton dress with lavender floral print, and a heavy cotton hooded cape. Jack discovered a pair of black leather boots, an off-white cotton shirt with long sleeves and scalloped collar, long cotton underwear, red knit cotton socks, calf-length brown wool pants with silk lining, and a duster-style heavy linen coat. Jack and Livi were positively nonplused by their discoveries.

Augustus stood beaming over the children. "Isn't this just lovely. Wonderful selections, Joshua! Wonderful indeed!" Augustus looked to the children, apparently waiting. For what, the children did not know. Not registering their dumbfounded expressions, Augustus exhorted them, "Well, get dressed, children. We must be off. Time is of the essence, you know."

Jack looked at Augustus skeptically. "You want us to put these on?"

Augustus, as though amused, responded, "Well of course, Jack. What else is there? Off you go."

At that moment, Augustus moved to what appeared to be a humidor resting upon an end table. He opened the lid to reveal a mechanism replete with dials and buttons. As he manipulated the instrument, two doors appeared on the outer wall of the library, replacing two adjacent windows. "Jack, you change in there, that's your room," Augustus said, indicating the door to his left as he faced it. "Olivia, your room is in there." He indicated the other door.

Jack bundled up his parcels and entered the designated room. As he did so, he recognized it to be the room that he was occupying in the actual house, though the furnishings were different. He recognized this to be another virtual room, noting the shimmering of objects in his peripheral vision. He presumed that Augustus had selected this room for him, having learned what rooms

Jack and Livi were occupying in the actual house. Jack marveled at the mysticism. "I've got to learn how to do this."

Jack looked at the clothes he had dropped upon his bed and determined that they weren't so bad. Particularly when compared to that which Livi would be wearing. He gave a small chuckle and began to disrobe. As he put on his new clothing, he decided that he would omit the long underwear. He felt certain that the boxer-briefs he was currently wearing would be just fine. When he finished dressing, he surveyed his reflection in the full-length mirror. His cotton shirt was somewhat blousy, putting him in mind of a pirate. His brown pants, which were actually quite comfortable, came over his boots to a level midway on his lower legs. He thought the look actually good. Satisfied, Jack grabbed up his coat and made for the door, backed out of his room and pulled the door behind him.

When he turned, he was startled to see that he was not in the library, but rather in the breakfast room. Like the room he had just left, it was furnished differently, but recognizable nonetheless. Augustus was sitting at the head of the table sipping coffee, and at just that moment Kingsley emerged from what Jack thought should be the kitchen, carrying a breakfast tray.

Augustus looked up over the paper he was reading. "Good morning, Jack. How about a touch of breakfast before we toddle along our way."

Jack's moment of confusion suddenly morphed into profound enlightenment. He knew he had not been asleep, but he was not tired. He felt as though he had just awakened from a peaceful sleep. He glanced at a table clock behind Augustus and saw that it indicated seven o'clock. He had come to understand that in the clock, time stood still. It could be manipulated, making the effects of the physiology of time on the body negligible. With a smile of revelation, Jack answered, "Breakfast would be great." Augustus looked at Jack with a knowing smile and a slight nodding of the head. He knew that Jack had realized one of the many mysteries of the clock.

As the three sat drinking coffee and chatting, Livi emerged from her room. Jack saw in her face the same initial surprise and ultimate realization that had transpired in his own mind. "Join us for breakfast, Olivia?" Augustus asked. After a slight pause, Livi answered, "I would love to." Augustus bestowed the same knowing smile upon her.

Livi looked younger than her age, wearing the blue flower-print dress that Kingsley procured. Her wardrobe, like Jack's, was not elegant, but rather utilitarian. She had donned the petticoat but left the remaining undergarments untouched, mainly because she did not know how to manipulate them. She carried the hooded cloak draped over her arm, and laid it upon the back of a vacant chair as she took her seat at the table.

Kingsley had prepared, or possibly procured, an elaborate breakfast feast. The four would-be time travelers discussed their ensuing adventure as they ate. Augustus reviewed that which they had discussed previously in regard to the journey. He cautioned that they would emerge in the 1835 library of Hollingsworth Manor, and would have to sneak out of the house unobserved. In 1835, Augustus was 23 years old. He, his wife and Kingsley were living in the manor at the time. Kingsley reported that he and the other servants generally would arise at five o'clock in the morning to begin morning chores. On Sunday, however, the house staff would sleep in till six o'clock. Therefore, the travelers would emerge at 5:30 on a Sunday morning.

"What about you, Lord Hollingsworth? What time did you get up back then?" asked Jack.

Kingsley smiled at Augustus, who immediately turned a light shade of crimson. Kingsley explained that Augustus would not be a problem at that time of day, as he was a newlywed and tended to stay in his chambers through the morning.

With their breakfast consumed and the table cleared, it was now time to embark upon what Jack and Livi felt was sure to be the grandest adventure of a lifetime. Augustus moved to a rather large breadbox that rested upon a side table in the breakfast room. He opened that lid to reveal once again the control mechanism of the room. He adjusted dials and pressed buttons as the room transformed back into the library. Augustus closed the lid of what was now the humidor, and addressed the travelers. "Joshua, will you be so kind as to enter the settings, please?"

Kingsley acknowledged Augustus with a slight bow and made his way over to the model clock, where he began to slide levers. Augustus, in turn, ambled over to a large armoire and opened it to reveal an assortment of cloaks, hats and wigs. As he rummaged through the cabinet, he explained rather nonchalantly to the children, "I'm afraid that I am going to have to make this journey incognito. It would stir quite a row if the townspeople were to recognize me, particularly looking ten years older than I should."

When he emerged from behind the door of the armoire, he sported a powdered wig and gold-rimmed glasses. He was dressed in a green coat with a black velvet collar, wore white trousers, and nestled an elaborate bamboo cane under his arm. "Are you quite ready, children?"

Jack and Livi, amazed at the remarkable transformation, responded wonderingly, "Yes."

With an air of excitement, Augustus exhorted them onward. "Then let us be off. There is no better time than the present to travel to the past." Augustus laughed at the pun, and redirected himself to Kingsley. "Joshua, lead the way, will you?"

"Of course," Kingsley replied. With a sweeping motion of his arm, Augustus indicated to the children to fall in line behind Kingsley. As Kingsley approached the clock, its door began to undulate, ultimately becoming a veil of light through which he disappeared. Jack went next, followed by Livi. Augustus brought up the rear. Jack and Livi, guided by Hollingsworth and Kingsley, were on their way to 1835 Colchester.

# CHAPTER 9

# Livi Meets Dickens

As the travelers ambled along the time passage, they had the perception that their surroundings were whirring past them, as if they were moving backwards though they were walking forward. Jack, who was directly behind Kingsley, watched him traverse the now familiar glowing curtain of light, disappearing to the other side. Jack approached the veil, hesitated but a moment, and held his breath as he stepped through.

Suddenly all motion stopped as though he had just stepped off a moving sidewalk. He found himself in the dark room that he recognized as the library of Hollingsworth Manor. As he tried to process the plethora of sensory stimulation, he was knocked forward when Livi emerged from the time portal, running into his back. Jack stumbled forward, banging into a table and catching a candelabrum just before it crashed to the floor. At that moment Augustus emerged, deftly sidestepped Livi whose hand had flown over her mouth in horror, and helped steady Jack. Augustus raised a finger to his lips, urging silence. Jack gently replaced the candelabrum onto the table and mouthed a silent "Sorry." Augustus nodded his forgiveness and looked toward Kingsley, who was already listening at the library door. Kingsley indicated that all was clear and lit a taper that he had retrieved from a candle box mounted on the door jam. As Jack, Livi and Augustus made their way toward Kingsley, Jack looked back at the portal. He noted that the large grandfather clock did not materialize as the shimmering veil gave way to a solid paneled wall. He made a mental note to ask Augustus about that.

Kingsley led the way out of the library into the evening parlor of the manor. Jack and Livi noted that most of the furnishings were the same as those in the present-day house. The troop walked silently as they approached the front door. Augustus motioned to the children to don their coats as he and Kingsley did the same. Satisfied that everyone was ready, Kingsley extinguished the taper and placed it in the candle box mounted at the front door. He quietly opened the door, allowing his three companions to emerge into the cool predawn of 1835 Colchester.

The surroundings of Hollingsworth Manor were barely recognizable to Jack and Livi. Though the house itself looked the same, the homes and shops that abutted the present-day manor were almost nonexistent. To the north they could see the edge of the town. But to the south, a vast expanse of undeveloped land occupied the area. The four travelers made their way down the front walk of the manor to the street below. They exited the gate and stepped onto the rutted dirt road that in the future would become the paved road of their neighborhood, Trinity Street.

Once the gate was closed behind them, Augustus felt it safe to speak. "Now, that wasn't so difficult, was it?" he queried jovially.

"No. Nothing to it," replied Jack, his heart still pounding in his throat. He then asked, "Lord Hollingsworth, where was the clock?"

Augustus looked at Jack quizzically. "The clock?"

"The grandfather clock. The time machine," Jack clarified.

"Oh, yes of course, the clock. Well, Jack, it hasn't been built yet, now has it?"

Jack pressed on, "Then how were we able to get here?"

"Ah, very good Jack," Augustus exclaimed. "The clock allows us to access the time portal, choosing when in time to travel. The portal itself is independent of the clock. It is the location of the portal that is important. It is consistent in location to the manor property, regardless of the historical time. Without a structure at the location, the portal's location is nigh impossible to identify. That is why we can only travel back to a time in which a structure of some form existed. Otherwise we may never find our way back! Wouldn't that be quite the predicament?"

Livi picked up the questioning as the group continued down the road. "So the portal stays open?"

"Oh no, no no no. When we set the portal for travel, it will remain open as long as the clock is wound and functioning. When we return to the clock and disengage the time travel settings, the portal closes."

Livi paused a moment in thought. "So, if the portal stays open when you are traveling, how do you keep someone from the past from entering the portal and traveling to the future?"

At that moment, Kingsley abruptly stopped and spun around to regard Augustus. Augustus too came to a halt, reciprocally regarding Kingsley. Livi and Jack walked a few steps more before registering that the other two had fallen back. They turned to Augustus, who began to stammer. "Well...that is to say...I mean of course...Oh my! It seems that I actually haven't accounted for that possibility. But, I assure you, that is very unlikely. After all, who would try to walk through a wall—right?" Augustus was not convinced by his own conclusion. The four continued on for a while in silence, Augustus brooding internally.

The four travelers, having turned down what would become Culver Street, continued west. Augustus wanted to skirt the periphery of the town before entering its center to avoid the populace, as it would appear suspicious for the group to be out at such an early hour. As they crossed over Head Street onto Church Street, they came upon a church that abutted a stone wall.

"What is that?" Livi asked Kingsley.

"Why, that is St. Mary of the Walls Church, Mistress Olivia," he said. The two stopped to admire the structure as Jack and Augustus sidled up next to them. "It doesn't look the same," Livi recognized, having seen a structure of that name in modern Colchester.

"You would not recognize this church, Olivia," declared Augustus. "It was demolished in 1870." Augustus regarded the building in silence. "Humpty Dumpty sat on the wall. Humpty Dumpty had a great fall. All the king's horses and all the king's men couldn't put Humpty together again." Augustus concluded the rhyme with an amused chuckle. Kingsley nodded knowingly; Jack and Livi eyed Augustus as though he had lost his mind. Turning to eye the children, Augustus noted their bemused gazes. "It is an old nursery rhyme, children."

Livi acknowledged, "Yes, we know it, but..."

Augustus surmised that the significance of the poem was lost upon them. Astounded that the children did not understand the reference, Augustus informed them: "This wall, children, is the wall from which Humpty Dumpty fell."

Jack looked skeptically at Augustus. "You mean an egg really fell off of the wall?"

Kingsley issued a chuckle, prompting Augustus to explain. "No, Jack, not an egg. A cannon."

Livi now regarded Augustus dubiously. "A cannon? Humpty Dumpty was a cannon?" she asked.

"A cannon indeed!" chortled Augustus. "Of course you two are familiar with the English Civil War, yes?" Livi affirmed her knowledge of the event; Jack was clueless.

Augustus continued: "Legend holds that in 1648, the Royalist forces loyal to the king were defending Colchester from a nearly three-month siege by the Roundheads. The famous sniper 'One-eyed' Thompson was manning the cannon, nicknamed Humpty Dumpty because of its large rounded shape, when the church tower was struck by enemy cannon fire. The tower collapsed, sending both Thompson and Humpty Dumpty to the ground. Neither the cavalry nor the infantry could mend the cannon. Thompson didn't fare too well either, for that matter. And there you have the origin of the rhyme. Colchester fell to the Roundheads soon after."

After a moment or two of silent contemplation, Augustus once again urged the travelers on. They turned north as dawn broke in full splendor. As they traveled, they saw farmers working their fields, but they were not noticed in turn. As they reached the northern limit of the township, they turned east onto what was already known as Northgate Street. They continued their stroll until they reached the northern entrance to the town. As they turned south to enter Colchester, travelers in carts and upon horseback passed them. They came upon other country dwellers who were walking into town. Along the way they exchanged pleasantries and salutations, the hour now being late enough that no oddity was perceived.

"I say. How about we head to the Red Lion for a bit of sustenance before we begin our exploration?" suggested Augustus.

"Sounds great to me!" replied Jack instantly, never one to turn down a meal. After a moment's consideration he questioned, "The Red Lion already exists? The same Red Lion as in our time?"

"Oh yes, dear boy," Augustus assured him. "The Red Lion has been in Colchester since the fifteenth century. So good to know it has still stood the test of time in your century."

As the travelers progressed south into the town, they passed by Colchester Castle. Jack noticed it first. "Hey look! It's the castle." As they made their way alongside the west wall and came into view of the main entrance at the keep's south side, they noticed men shackled together, being led out of the castle. They were being loaded onto carts, which were lined up along the front.

"Lord Hollingsworth, what's going on?" asked Livi.

"Why, I don't know," responded Augustus. "But I shall ascertain." With that, Augustus broke away from the group and moved toward a man whom he perceived to be in charge of the maneuver by virtue of the bellowing of profanities he directed at both the prisoners and the guards. When the head jailer saw Augustus approaching, his demeanor changed into that of a consummate professional. He tipped his hat as he addressed Augustus and grinned a rotted smile. "Good morning, sir. How may I be of service to you on this glorious morn?"

Augustus returned the greeting and questioned the happenings. "I say, my good man, what exactly is transpiring here?"

The jailer looked at Augustus in dismay. "You must not be from around here, mate," he concluded. "Colchester jail is closing. I'm moving all of these blokes to the new jail to continue their incarceration."

Augustus, realizing that he should have remembered this, was thankful that the jailer was of little intelligence. "Ah yes, of course. Well done, sir. I shall report that you have the matter well in hand." The jailer, now sure that Augustus was some royal official, bowed deeply and uttered his appreciation and devotion to the Crown.

Augustus rejoined the group, and Jack pumped him for an explanation. "So what's happening? What are they doing?"

"It appears that they are closing the jail."

Jack, being enthralled with the castle, pressed on. "Can we go see it?"

Augustus pondered a moment. "I tell you what, Jack. Let's come back and see it when it was truly impressive. When we get back home, you pick the date and that will be our next journey."

"Whoa, that will be cool!" Jack opined.

They continued south into the heart of Colchester. At the High Street they turned west and walked until they arrived at the Red Lion Inn. Had they gone just a bit farther south, they would have been back at Hollingsworth Manor, having nearly gone full circle. The Red Lion Inn looked amazingly similar to its modern counterpart. Like Hollingsworth Manor, the inn was constructed in timber-frame fashion with the second floor jutting past the first and the third past the second. Timber beams accented the façade, and the wooden placard bearing the familiar image of the red painted lion standing upon its back legs hung prominently from the second floor above the entryway.

As the four prepared to go inside, Augustus retrieved his moneybag and inspected its contents. Satisfied that he had indeed procured currency appropriate for the time, he gleefully announced that it was time to "break fast." Kingsley stepped forward and opened the large front door, which also bore an etched glass image of a lion raised upon its hind legs, poised for attack. Augustus ushered the children in and followed behind them. It was but a moment later that Jack realized that Kingsley had remained outside.

"Where is Mr. Kingsley? Why didn't he come in?" he asked.

Augustus appeared uncomfortable. "Let's sit, Jack, and I'll explain."

The dining hall of the Red Lion Inn was floored in rough-hewn oak, scattered upon which were tables of various sizes and shapes. An open fireplace was situated at one end of the long room and emitted a stifling hot combustion. To make matters worse, the dining hall was packed with tables and patrons. Augustus found a table at the end of the hall opposite the fireplace where ventilation was adequate, and directed the children to sit. After having been brought a pot of coffee (rather bad coffee, Jack noted), Augustus spoke.

"Slavery in the United Kingdom was abolished in 1833. In 1835 Colchester, emancipation still was not terribly popular. Men of color, though free, were not equal. It took a number of years before they were readily accepted into society as free men. Joshua has gone around back and will eat in the kitchen." Augustus paused, visibly unnerved. "These were not pleasant times for Joshua and his people."

The three ate, the children hurriedly as they wanted to reconnect with Kingsley as soon as possible. It was as they were finishing their meal that it happened. A young gentleman dressed in business attire entered the dining hall. "Well, there you are! We should have been at the assembly twenty minutes ago!" The gentleman pronounced this to another man who was sitting at a corner table, three down from the time travelers. He was reading a newspaper. As the first man approached this table, the newspaper was lowered to reveal a clean-shaven young man with an olive complexion and chestnut-colored wavy hair. Livi immediate recognized him as the young Charles Dickens, and her hand flew to her mouth to stifle a gasp.

Dickens gave the man a satirical smile. "Sit, Joseph, join me in coffee."

Joseph regarded Dickens for a moment. In an act of resignation, he pulled out the opposite chair and plopped into it. "Charles, why are you here? The aldermen have already assembled."

Dickens emitted a chuckle as he shook his head. "Joseph, you need to relax. You know full well that no business will be discussed for at least another twenty minutes. Here, read the Chronicle." Dickens slid his copy of the paper for which he reported over to Joseph and signaled the waiter for another cup, which was readily produced. Dickens then poured coffee for his friend and fellow reporter.

Livi, having taken this all in, was awestruck. It took a moment for Jack to realize that she was not engaged in the conversation of their table, but rather appeared to be a million miles away. "Livi, did you hear me? What's the matter with you?" he asked.

Livi, keeping her eyes trained on Dickens, lowered her hand from her mouth. "It's him. It's Charles Dickens."

Augustus and Jack both looked in the direction of Livi's gaze and saw the pair of men. "Which one is he?" Jack asked.

"The handsome one," Livi replied dreamily.

Jack surveyed the scene again for a moment. "Which one is the handsome one?"

Livi now looked at Jack, who in turn kept his eye on the two men. "The one on the left, Jack," she said with some degree of exasperation.

"Are you quite sure, Olivia?" asked Augustus.

"Absolutely sure," Livi affirmed. "I recognize him from his portrait at the museum. And I heard the other man call him Charles," she added.

In the meantime, Joseph had not picked up the paper or drunk the coffee that Dickens poured, but continued to plead with his friend. "Charles, if you don't get this story in to London by tomorrow, Sir Scott will have your head."

Dickens regarded his friend with amusement. "Joseph, you worry to excess. In any event, Sir Scott adores me." Then, seeing that his friend was truly unnerved, he graciously relented. "Come, let us go before you fall prostrate." Dickens rose from his chair, dropped some coins on the table, and moved for the door. With a sigh of relief, Joseph followed.

Livi's gaze followed Dickens as he made his way to the door. Though she was blatantly staring at him, Charles Dickens did not notice the awestruck girl. When the door closed behind Dickens and his friend Joseph, Livi spoke with animated excitement. "That was him, Lord Hollingsworth! That was Charles Dickens!"

"Indeed it appears so," replied Augustus.

"I can't believe I actually saw him," Livi sighed.

"I don't see what's so special about the guy," observed Jack.

Livi retorted as though her best friend had been slighted, "He's only the greatest author of the Victorian age, Jack!" Jack shrugged, utterly unimpressed.

Augustus took in the exchange with a wistful smile upon his face. It had been a long time since he had enjoyed such spirited discourse. "Well, Olivia, I should think you not content to leave it at that. Let's gather up Joshua and catch up to the ole chap."

"Can we?" asked Livi, intrigued by the possibility.

"Well, of course. He's off to report upon the Assembly. He should be easy enough to find." Augustus stood, walked around to Livi and offered his arm to help her up. "Shall we then, Mistress?"

"Absolutely!" replied Livi. Augustus too placed some coins upon the table, turned and escorted Livi to the door. As the two made their way outside, Jack took the last biscuit from the tray, shoved it into his mouth and scurried after them.

Kingsley was leaning against a hitching rail, patiently waiting for his companions when the three emerged. Livi ran toward him and related the excitement of their breakfast sighting of Charles Dickens. Kingsley reveled in her enthusiasm, truly happy for the joy Livi was experiencing. "And Lord Hollingsworth said we can go find him! He's reporting on the aldermen's assembly!"

Kingsley looked to Augustus, who in turn nodded knowingly. It was understood between the two of them that Jack and Livi were discovering the magic of the time machine. "Then we should be off, Mistress Olivia. We don't want to miss him, now do we?"

Livi became suddenly frantic. "Oh my gosh, we need to hurry. What if we do miss him?" Kingsley and Augustus laughed. "No need to worry, Olivia. Remember, time is on our side," Augustus reassured her. Jack regarded Livi as though she were a groupie of a boy band. He had never seen this side of his sister before. He wasn't sure what to make of it.

When the troop arrived at the Assembly Hall, they found a throng of people packed around the entrance. To Jack, the exterior of the hall looked like a church. The travelers pushed through the crowd and into the door. The aldermen occupied the center of the room, sitting in small desks arranged in rows and columns, senior members to the front, junior members toward the back, and the two political parties segregated on either side. The desks faced a dais upon which the president of the assembly sat, abutted by the senior party leaders of the assembly and support staff. Today's assembly was an open forum, resulting in an aggregate of the population of Colchester being packed into the hall, lining its walls. Livi, Jack, Hollingsworth and Kingsley squeezed themselves into the back of the hall, Livi straining to spy Dickens. She found him standing against the wall to her left, scribbling furiously upon a pad. With disappointment, she determined that it would be impossible to get any further through the crowd to approach him.

After five minutes of discourse from the aldermen, Jack announced that he was thoroughly bored. Kingsley suggested that he and Jack might better enjoy exploring Colchester, perhaps making an excursion to the castle. In an instant, Jack spun around, announced "See ya'll

later," and bolted out the door, Kingsley happily following behind. Livi and Augustus remained in the hall, entranced by the discussion and its historic significance.
In no time it seemed, hours passed and the president
announced that the assembly would recess for the mid-
day meal. With that, the crowd began to exit the hall,
Livi and Augustus caught in the tide that washed out
of the hall and onto the lawn. Once outside, the crowd
dispersed.

Livi looked forlornly at Augustus. "I don't know
where he went."

Augustus looked about, also unable to locate Dickens.
"Well, Olivia, he can't have gotten far. I shall walk
around this way. You go around the other side. I'm certain we will locate him." The two set off around the assembly hall in different directions in their quest to locate
Charles Dickens.

Only a few moments later Livi once again encountered Dickens. As she made the corner to walk along the
side of the assembly hall, Livi spied Dickens and Joseph.
They were just at that moment taking an outdoor seat at
a small bistro across the street from the hall. Livi stopped
dead in her tracks with her mouth agape. She was literally frozen, uncertain how to proceed. After a few moments she realized that she was standing conspicuously
in the middle of the sidewalk. Upon that realization, she
ducked behind the pole of a kerosene streetlamp and
stared, unwittingly just as conspicuous as she was before. She watched as Dickens and Joseph again drank

coffee and ate small sandwiches, noting Joseph to be much more at ease than he was earlier in the day. All the while, Dickens was making notations upon his tablet. Suddenly, Joseph jumped up from his chair at the recognition of one of the senior aldermen making his way to the door of the bistro. He engaged for a moment in animated conversation with the gentleman, before turning to Dickens and gesturing furiously for him to come over and join the discourse. Dickens, in turn, amicably acquiesced as he laid his quill upon the pad and slowly ambled toward the two men.

As if in a trance, Livi was drawn to the now abandoned table. In an instant, she found herself reaching over the garden rail that sequestered the bistro tables from the sidewalk and taking hold of the tablet upon which Dickens had been writing. She marveled at the notion that she was actually reading the writings of Dickens in his own hand. She flipped through the pages, coming to the last, where she saw Dickens' pen name with which she was now so familiar: "Boz." As she traced her finger over the word, she was startled by the voice and looming presence of Charles Dickens who, having come to the street side of the rail, was standing by her side.

"Would you be so kind as to explain what it is that you are doing with my tablet, young lady?"

Livi was nonplused and once again froze in indecision. Dickens spoke again. "Well, what do you have to say for yourself?"

Still Livi had no reply. "Very well, I think a visit to the constable is in order. Come with me." With that, Dickens grabbed Livi's arm with one hand, retrieved his tablet with the other, and began to walk with her onto the street.

Joseph raced up to the pair, having witnessed the interchange. "Charles, what are you doing?"

Dickens kept pace as he responded, "This little street urchin is a thief. I am bringing her to the authorities."

Joseph, trying to keep up with the two, spoke with nervous laughter. "Charles, surely you don't think this girl a thief. What has she stolen?"

Still walking, Dickens declared matter-of-factly, "She stole my tablet."

Joseph grabbed Dickens by the arm and halted his progress. "Charles, thieves don't steal tablets! Of what value is that?" He then turned to Livi. "What is your name, dear?"

Livi finally found her voice. "Olivia, and I wasn't stealing your tablet, Mr. Dickens. I was just reading it. I'm a big fan of yours!"

Dickens looked at her confusedly. "You are a what?"

Livi now spoke with enthusiasm. "I'm a fan. I've read all of your works. My absolute favorite is..." Livi was stopped midsentence by the voice of Augustus booming as he crossed the street toward the group. Augustus had finally rounded the Assembly Hall when he saw the three in discussion, and surmised that nothing good would come from it.

"There you are! I didn't know where you had gone. You are to stay with me at all times, young lady. There will be repercussions, I'll have you know." Augustus was now upon the trio. "Gentlemen, I am terribly sorry. I'm afraid my charge has wandered away from me. I assure you, she is completely harmless."

Dickens looked upon Augustus skeptically. "And who are you, sir?"

Augustus hesitated. "Who am I?"

Dickens was becoming exasperated. "Yes, who are you and what is your relationship to this girl?"

Augustus composed himself. "I am Brown. Brownlow. Augustus Brownlow. I am the custodian of this unfortunate orphan."

Joseph looked at Livi. "You are an orphan, dear?"

Livi glanced toward Augustus as she answered, "I guess so." Joseph did not register the uncertainty. "Charles, the poor child is an orphan."

Augustus jumped in. "Yes, we are passing through on our way to London, where she will be deposited in the London Orphan Asylum. You will not be troubled by her again, sir, I assure you."

Livi looked Dickens in the eye as she addressed him. "Mr. Dickens, I wasn't stealing. I just love your writing."

Dickens regarded the group, and then spoke: "Very well, Olivia. Go about your way, and take this." Dickens presented Livi with his tablet.

Livi was astounded. "Really? I can have your tablet?"

Dickens, not wanting to reveal his sentimentality, cleared his throat and firmed his tone. "Yes, yes, take it and be off with you. I'm very busy."

Livi took the tablet and embraced Dickens. "Thank you."

Dickens hesitantly patted her back. "You are welcome."

Livi released him and bade him farewell as she and Augustus turned and walked away. Dickens followed the pair with his gaze, a smile upon his face. Joseph spoke, breaking his reverie. "Well, that was certainly a twist for you, Charles."

Dickens looked at Joseph, an idea forming in his mind. "Hmm, let me see your tablet."

Joseph handed over his tablet. Dickens turned to a blank page and scribbled: Olivia Twist - orphan, thief. He tore the page out of the tablet, folded it, inserted it into his waistcoat pocket, and returned to his table with Joseph.

# CHAPTER 10

# The Witch Hunter

Back in the library, Livi prattled incessantly as Augustus sat across from her in a high wingback chair, taking in her excitement, her enthusiasm. Kingsley fussed about in the presentation of afternoon tea. He too listened to Livi's animated discourse as she recounted every detail of her adventure with Dickens, noting all the while that she clutched the author's tablet as though it might fly away of its own accord. Jack, however, sat apart from the group. He was engrossed in a book. His face was set in determination and seemed to reveal a heretofore-unseen scowl. Augustus glanced toward Jack from time to time, and attributed the foreign expression to the flickering light of the fireplace. Somehow, though, he thought there was something more.

Jack was in fact reading a book that detailed the atrocities of the infamous witch hunter, Matthew Hopkins. In the course of his many excursions to the Colchester

Castle Museum, Jack was inexplicably drawn to the witch hunter. He couldn't help but read more and more about him. And he couldn't help but loathe him more and more. Jack didn't understand why he was so drawn by the villain. The acts of cruelty of which he learned disturbed him almost to the point of physical illness. Still, he had to know all that he could about the wretch. Jack had an agenda, an agenda that he shared with no one.

"Jack, dear boy, why don't you come join us for tea?" Augustus had become a bit concerned by Jack's determined reading and felt a distraction was in order. Jack was startled back to his surroundings. "Oh, sure, that sounds great." He marked his place in the book and replaced it upon the shelf.

"What are you reading so intently, Jack?" asked Augustus.

Jack was intentionally vague. "Oh, just brushing up on seventeenth-century Colchester. You know, just to be prepared."

"Ah, very good, Jack, very good!" replied Augustus, relieved to know that Jack's determination was a desire to be prepared for tomorrow's travel. "One can never be too prepared, isn't that right, Joshua."

Kingsley nodded in agreement, "Indeed so." Joshua too had noted Jack's behavior when he was "researching" the time of travel he had chosen. Kingsley's concern was not so easily assuaged.

As Jack settled himself to tea, Augustus queried, "So Master Jack, what have you decided? What shall be our destination tomorrow?"

Jack paused as if considering his options, knowing full well where he planned to go. "How about the castle? That's as good a place as any to start."

Augustus smiled. "Right you are! The castle it is, then."

The afternoon progressed and supper was had. As the evening waned, Jack continued his research, staying up long after the others had retired for the night. Augustus had primed the travelers as to what to expect when they exited the time portal into 1647 Colchester. At that time, Hollingsworth Manor consisted only of the main house, that being the front section. The wing housing the library had not yet been constructed. Augustus cautioned that the travelers would emerge outside of the house and would have to mark the exact location of the portal to return. He assured that each traveler had appropriate period clothing and currency. Before turning in to bed himself, he admonished Jack not to stay up too long, as he would need to be well rested for the next day's adventure.

The next morning, the travelers did indeed emerge directly into the cool predawn air outside of Hollingsworth Manor. Kingsley was first through; he stretched a length of braided twine across the site of the portal entry and staked it firmly into place. The others emerged in short order and, as on their previous journey, hustled to the street, a muddied trail really, and circumvented the village until an acceptable morning hour was reached. Jack and Livi were surprised to hear that they would once again breakfast at the Red Lion. Having been built in 1465, the hostelry was quite familiar and functional in 1647. As before, Kingsley was relegated to having his meal behind the building, thus prompting the remaining three to hastily consume their nourishment. Fed and rested except for Jack, who was fatigued as he did not heed Augustus' instruction to be mindful of the late hour, the travelers set off for the castle.

As they approached it, the group witnessed a different bustle of activity than they had from the previous day's travel. A large throng of people was congregated on the grounds behind the castle, apparently consumed with some activity along the bank of the River Colne. "My word, what in the world could be going on there?" asked Augustus aloud. "Perhaps some festival activity. Is there a festival, Joshua?"

Kingsley was quite dubious. "I know of no festivals at this time of year in 1647 Colchester, Augustus. Perhaps we should divert our course and return later."

"Why so, Joshua?" queried Augustus.

But before Kingsley could answer, Jack forcefully interjected, "No! We need to see what's going on."

The three traveling companions were taken aback by Jack's determination, but Augustus cautiously conceded. "Very well, Jack, we'll take a look. Lead the way."

As they walked, Livi asked Jack in hushed tones, "Jack, do you know what's happening down there?"

Continuing in his determined gait, Jack responded, "I think so. I think it's Hopkins."

The name did resonate with Livi, but she couldn't place its context. "Hopkins? Who's that?"

With undisguised malice, Jack clarified: "Matthew Hopkins, the Witchfinder General." Livi then remembered. Jack had spoken of Hopkins each time he returned from the castle museum. She had no real interest in the character, and never accompanied Jack to the exhibit that detailed the witch-hunting activities of East Anglia. She did know, however, that Jack spoke with disdain of the man and his nefarious activities.

What Jack knew of Matthew Hopkins was that he began his reign of terror in 1644, during the turmoil of the English Civil War. He claimed to be commissioned by Parliament to uncover and prosecute witches. Hopkins discovered that he could exploit the Witchcraft Act of 1563 and prey upon the fear and ignorance of villagers by extorting large sums of money in exchange for ridding their communities of "witches." Hopkins became very wealthy, extracting up to 20 pounds of silver per township. This was a large sum of money, considering the average wage of a villager was about two pennies a day. In the course of his career, Hopkins was responsible for over 200 executions of innocent souls. Some authorities place the number closer to 400. Though torture was outlawed in England during Hopkins' tenure, he circumvented such inconvenience, subjecting targeted townspeople to sleep deprivation, near drowning, repetitive puncturing with needles, and other atrocities designed to extract confessions and accusations of "accomplices."

Jack had learned that two of Hopkins' favorite tests were the elucidation of the devil's mark, and the swim test. The devil's mark was a supposed area on the body of a witch that was numb to feeling and would not bleed when punctured. Hopkins would have his henchman John Stearne pierce the victim with needles, causing a great deal of unrelenting pain. Once Hopkins felt the victim to have been adequately tortured, he would take his knife and thrust it into the accused. Hopkins' knife, however, had a retractable blade and would not pierce the skin, thus confirming the devil's mark and proving the accused a witch. The swim test was based upon the belief that a witch would be rejected by water, as water was used for baptism and a witch was a consort of the devil. The accused would have hands and feet bound together and would be lowered into the water. If they sank, they were innocent. If they floated, having been rejected by the water, then they were confirmed a witch and condemned to death by hanging. Jack never understood how it was that Hopkins had so much success in garnering convictions by this test. Surely, he thought, anyone bound in such a way would sink!

As Jack led the way behind the castle to the riverbank, the bustle of activity became harried. Though it was clear by the crowd's demeanor that whatever was happening was not a happy occurrence, the throng of on-lookers was too thick to allow the travelers visual access to the event ongoing. Livi, having now become quite tentative, grasped Jack by the arm, causing him to abruptly stop and spin toward her. "Jack, what is going on down there? You know, don't you?"

Jack could tell by Livi's tone and gaze that she was frightened. Still, he didn't want to voice his thoughts. Augustus, fully in tune now with Livi's concern, addressed Jack. "Jack, do you have an idea of what is happening? Is there some reason that you specifically wanted to come here?"

Jack hesitated, but quickly realized he would now have to state his intentions. "I believe it's Hopkins. I believe it's a witch trial," he admitted. Jack then explained to his three travel companions all that he had learned about Matthew Hopkins and the witch hunts of East Anglia. He explained the atrocities that Hopkins committed. He revealed that his motive was to put an end to Hopkins' reign of terror.

Augustus now understood the reason for Jack's distraction the night before. "Jack, dear boy. What little I know of the witch hunts in Colchester, I know to have been horrible. I know they were unjust and cruel. I understand that. But I also understand that history is history. We are here to observe. You know that we cannot do anything to alter the events of the past. I've explained that to you. You understand that, don't you?"

Jack did understand, at least in his mind. But his heart told another truth. His heart told him that Hopkins had to be stopped. Jack also realized, just at this moment, that he didn't have a plan to stop Hopkins. He was just a kid. What could he do, anyway?

As Jack was coming to the realization of his limitations, a group of three women approached from the riverbank, obviously distraught. Kingsley addressed them with a polite bow and inquired of them, "I beg your pardon, ladies. Can you tell us what is transpiring down below?"

The women stopped and one cried, "That devil Hopkins has just convicted Pastor Lowe. That poor old man is not a witch. John Lowe is a man of God!"

Augustus asked, "How was he convicted?"

Another of the women answered, "Hopkins has kept him awake for days, making him walk his cell incessantly. His feet are blistered and bloodied. Hopkins swam him in the river and he rose to the surface."

The third woman then added her sentiments. "He is now bringing Pastor Lowe to the gallows. He won't even allow him the benefit of clergy. The poor soul is reciting his own burial rite!" With that, the woman burst into tears and her two companions led her away.

Jack became enraged. Trying to contain his anger, his eyes welled with tears. Livi had never see him in such a state and moved to console him. As she tried to embrace him, Jack pulled away.

"No, Livi! This isn't right! He can't do this!" Livi looked Jack in the eye and, with compassion she had never felt before, tried to reason with him. "Jack, there is nothing we can do. There's nothing anyone can do. History has to run its course."

Kingsley agreed. "Master Jack, Olivia is right. We cannot change the events of history. Perhaps we should return to the manor and plan another venture." Jack considered for a moment, looking down at his feet. Then with a determined gaze, he fixed his eyes on Kingsley's. "We have to do something." Jack then turned and calmly walked toward the crowd.

Augustus addressed Kingsley, "Joshua, take Livi back to the manor. I shall go after Jack and bring him forthwith." Augustus then turned and followed after Jack.

"Come, Mistress Olivia. Lord Hollingsworth will garner Master Jack home safely." Kingsley led Livi away as she repeatedly glanced over her shoulder after Jack and Hollingsworth.

Jack did not race away from the others. He walked deliberately. He was on a mission. He had learned so much of Matthew Hopkins that he felt he knew him, and despised every fiber of the infamous man's being. Jack entered the throng with Augustus close behind, calling after him. Jack, however, being slight of build easily slipped through the crowd, soon leaving Hollingsworth trapped behind the barrier of humanity. As Jack reached the front of the crowd, he saw a ragged-appearing man slip and fasten the noose about another man's neck.

Also standing upon the platform with his back to the crowd was a man dressed in what to Jack appeared to be a Pilgrim's costume, replete with tall hat and long cloak. He intuited that man to be Matthew Hopkins and quickly surmised that the hangman was his henchman, John Stearne.

Jack watched paralyzed by the surreal nature of what he was witnessing. He felt as though he were dreaming. Before Jack could completely process the circumstances, he heard the reverberation of the wooden trap door slamming into the balustrade of the gallows, followed by the sight of John Lowe plummeting down, only to be abruptly halted in his fall by the tautness of the rope from which his corpse now dangled. In the very next instant Jack heard a scream of agony followed by a plethora of profanities directed at Hopkins. It was when Hopkins turned and glared at him with pure malice that Jack realized he was the source of exuberant rebuke. Matthew Hopkins slowly descended the makeshift stairway from the gallows, all the while keeping his piercing stare upon Jack. Jack felt the crowd dissipate, leaving nothing but air between him and Hopkins. At this moment he did not feel frightened. In fact, he was rather confused. The man approaching him, whom he was certain was Hopkins, appeared to be little more than a boy himself. In all of the drawings Jack had seen, Hopkins was portrayed as an old man. But Matthew Hopkins was in fact only in his mid-twenties. Not at all what Jack had expected.

As Hopkins approached, Jack was startled by a strong grasp upon his shoulder. He turned to see Augustus, who appeared quite concerned. "Come, Jack, we should be off now."

As Hollingsworth made to lead Jack back into the crowd and away from Hopkins, a deep baritone voice boomed a command: "Stop where you are, sir!" Hopkins' voice did not match his boyish countenance. "Is this insidious child yours, sir?" Hopkins was now well upon the two.

"He is my ward," Augustus responded.

Hopkins raised his cane and brought it down hard upon the back of Jack's leg, causing him to fall to the ground with a cry of pain. The act was so sudden and unexpected that Augustus failed to intervene. But when Hopkins made to strike Jack again as he commented upon his insolence, Augustus grasped Hopkins' arm, causing the attacker to grimace. "You shall not strike the boy again," declared Hollingsworth, and he deftly twisted Hopkins' arm behind his back, forcing him to the ground. In an instant Stearne was upon Augustus, pummeling him from behind. Hopkins, now free of Augustus' grasp, instructed the nearby guards: "Arrest this man! He has laid hands upon the Witchfinder General!"

As the guards rousted Hollingsworth to his feet, Stearne pulled a small whip from behind his back and began to lash Augustus. Jack leapt from the ground and launched himself upon Stearne's back in an attempt to stop the assault. Stearne, a rather burly man, easily shook Jack off. Jack flew through the air and landed with a thud upon his back, knocking the wind out of his lungs. Stearne moved toward Jack, whip upraised.

Augustus, unable to free himself, called out "Jack! Run!" Jack scampered backward as he caught his breath, rolled to his hands and knees and bolted into the crowd.

"Quickly, Jack!" Augustus yelled after him as Jack sprinted away.

Stearne turned back toward Augustus to continue the beating. His progress was interrupted by Hopkins' booming voice. "You fool! After the boy! Bring him to me!" For an instant Stearne was dazed and confused, which was not an unusual state for him. He would much rather beat a prisoner than chase a simple boy. "Go, you simpleton!" ordered Hopkins.

Stearne turned and lumbered into the crowd. Inasmuch as the townspeople parted to allow Jack's egress, they seemed to consolidate as Stearne tried to push his way through. Ultimately, with bludgeoning and curses, Stearne penetrated the mass and emerged to see Jack rounding the castle. Not a particularly agile or fast man, Stearne was pleased to see that the boy was hobbled by a limp. Perhaps he would catch him after all.

Jack was a moving mass of pure adrenaline. Though his knee was swollen, he couldn't feel the pain. All he knew was that he wasn't moving as quickly as he would like. Jack glanced over his shoulder as he ran, noting that Stearne was closing the distance. Jack was well onto what he knew as the High Street. He darted across a grassy field, heading toward Hollingsworth Manor. He passed in front of the house on Trinity Street until he was at the south side.

Jack hopped over the low retaining wall and made his way toward the portal. Stearne was close behind. For a moment, Jack became disoriented. Where was the portal? He paused for a moment to visualize where the future library would be. As he scanned back farther from the street, he saw the cord that Kingsley had staked into the ground. Jack bolted for it. As Stearne rounded the house he saw the boy run and leap as if jumping over a ditch. He watched Jack disappear into a glimmering light. Stearne cautiously approached the area, walking with his hands outstretched as if trying to feel an invisible mass. Stearne saw the twine cord staked into the ground. He walked between it and the manor, stooped down and felt it. There was nothing odd in its texture. He stood and passed his hand over the cord, but discovered nothing unusual. He then walked around the cord to the other side. Again Stearne brought his hand over the cord. This time, however, he felt a cold mist and saw his hand disappear into the light.

# CHAPTER 11

# The Castle Prison

Augustus was quite put out by the impertinence with which he was being treated. He was unaccustomed to being bustled and roughly thrown about. But then again, he had never involved himself in fisticuffs. Perhaps his subsequent treatment was the natural consequence. In any event, he certainly would not have allowed Hopkins to strike the boy again. So, his actions were worth the current predicament in which he found himself. He was sure that Kingsley would be along shortly to secure his release.

He hoped that his friend's arrival would come sooner rather than later, as the hay that lined his cell floor had the most unpleasant stench of stale urine. He was uncertain if it was from the goats or the drunks with whom he shared the ground floor cell in the Colchester Castle keep. He surmised that it was probably a product of the drunks, as the goats seemed much better mannered. The fleas that danced upon his skin he also surmised to have originated from the drunks, having abandoned them in search of a less toxic host.

Augustus had been charged with the crime of assault upon a Parliamentary official. He was told that the sheriff would be in the village sometime within the month to formally charge him. His jailer, however, suggested that a fine might well supplant the need to involve the sheriff, if Augustus could arrange such. Augustus felt quite sure that when Joshua arrived, he would have sufficient funds to make the bribe. In the meanwhile, Augustus was resigned to sitting in the corner of his cell well away from both goats and drunks, his handkerchief pressed against his nose to filter the foul smell. He busied himself by swatting at the fleas and other insects that sought refuge upon his body from the rotting hay.

Colchester Castle in 1647 was a functioning jail. The castle complex, completed in 1101, consisted of a large defended enclosure in which were a number of outbuildings and, in the center, the fortified palace of the king, the castle keep. The keep itself measured 150 feet by 110 feet, making it the largest Norman keep in Britain, even larger than the famous Tower of London. In 1647, however, the defensive enclosure and surrounding buildings of the castle bailey were for the most part gone.

Augustus noticed that the keep had three levels in contrast to the two that remained during his time. He thought he remembered that the upper story was demolished in the seventeenth century, but it was not clear to him why. Augustus was celled on the ground floor, which also housed the guardroom and the armory. Both were well secured from the jail area. Augustus had been brought in from the main entrance on the ground level at the south side of the keep. Within the southeast buttress of the keep was a spiral staircase that ascended to the first floor and descended into what he presumed to be a basement. The jail cells were arranged on the west side of the keep, and the guardroom and armory on the east. For the moment, this was all that Augustus knew of the castle. He felt that this was enough, having no desire to learn more as morning morphed into afternoon and afternoon into evening. *What is keeping Kingsley so?* thought Augustus, remembering that Joshua was interminably slow.

Jack felt as though his traversal through the portal was taking a lifetime. Never before had the images appeared to move so slowly by him. Jack's heart was racing. He couldn't believe that his plan, though now he saw how ill conceived it was, had resulted in the arrest of Augustus Hollingsworth.

When Jack finally emerged into the virtual library, he saw Livi and Kingsley waiting pensively. When Livi saw Jack, she bolted from her chair, ran toward him and wrapped him in an embrace. "Jack, thank God you're back. Are you okay?"

Jack for his part had never felt so safe as he did now in the arms of his sister. "I'm fine, Livi." He savored the moment until Kingsley jolted him back to reality with his inquiry. "Master Jack, where is Lord Hollingsworth?"

Jack slowly released Livi as he turned to Kingsley. "He's been arrested." Jack recounted the events that transpired after Kingsley and Livi had left. When he told how John Stearne had pursued him, Kingsley became nervous.

"Master Jack, did Stearne see you pass through the portal?"

Jack contemplated for a moment. "No, no he didn't see me. I'm sure that I lost him. I was through before he made it around the house."

Kingsley glanced suspiciously at the clock. "Are you sure, Master Jack?"

Jack, now racking his memory, replied, "Yeah, I'm sure. It took me a couple of seconds to find the portal, but I didn't see him when I went through. I don't think he could have seen me."

"Very well, Master Jack," Kingsley stated. "We shall hope not."

Livi was now quite concerned. "What are we going to do, Mr. Kingsley?"

"We are going to retrieve Lord Hollingsworth, of course!" replied Kingsley. "This isn't the first time Augustus has gotten himself into a precarious circumstance. I'm quite used to extricating him from unpleasant situations. In fact, it wasn't long ago that I had to rescue him from Queen Victoria!" Kingsley recalled with a chuckle.

"Queen Victoria?" Livi was certain that she had not heard correctly.

"Indeed, the Queen herself! Come, let us lunch and I will tell you all about it."

Kingsley went over to the humidor and adjusted the settings so that the virtual informal dining room materialized. Jack was a bit taken aback. "Don't you think we should go get Lord Hollingsworth, Mr. Kingsley?"

Kingsley looked at Jack with amusement. "He'll be fine, Master Jack. As I said, this isn't the first time. In any event, we must eat and we do have time on our side." Kingsley motioned the children to the table. "Sit, children, while I procure sustenance."

Kingsley disappeared into the kitchen area, and returned shortly with a tray of sandwiches and a pitcher of lemonade. After he served the children, Kingsley sat at the table, made a plate for himself, and began to relate the story of Hollingsworth and Queen Victoria.

"So let me tell you about Augustus and Queen Victoria. As you know, Augustus has always been fascinated with timepieces. What you don't know is that he is also quite enamored with trains. Augustus wanted to ride the first train from Colchester to London. Unfortunately, the inaugural run was made in 1843, while we were traveling in France. So Augustus and I went back to 1843 and boarded that first train from Colchester to London. Augustus was in heaven. He was like a child in his excitement. When we arrived in London, he decided he was going to meet Queen Victoria who, like him, was also a great fan of the locomotive.

"Victoria was in the sixth year of her reign. I, of course, told him that it would be near impossible to have an audience with her, which only made him more determined. So, off we went to Buckingham Palace. Augustus posed as an art dealer, knowing of Victoria's love for art, and was granted admittance into the royal gallery. I was in the atrium with a large group of others when the Queen and her entourage swept into the gallery. Augustus was granted an audience and was admitted into the Queen's private studio. A few moments passed and the Queen's attendants emerged. But, the Queen and Augustus did not come out. Hours passed and the people waiting with me in the atrium filtered away, one by one. Finally, night fell and the late hour wore on; still no Queen and no Augustus. Apparently I had fallen asleep, because at just around midnight I heard a frantic knock upon the window by which I was sitting. I was startled awake to find the silhouette of a man on the ledge outside. I hastened to open the window, revealing the man to be Augustus perched upon the ledge, completely naked. I ushered him through the window, pulled down one of the window's drapes, wrapped him in it, and hurried him out of the castle."

Jack and Livi listened with their jaws dropped. Livi was the first to come to her senses. "Why was he on the ledge? And why was he naked?"

Kingsley laughed. "Well, it turns out that Victoria is not as prudish as her reputation suggests. Victoria is an art lover, which is well known. But, she is particularly appreciative of nudes. In fact, her passion was to paint nudes--nude men specifically. Apparently the Queen was expecting a model at the time Augustus and I made our visit. She mistook Augustus for that model. The actual model was turned away soon after Augustus and the Queen retreated to her studio. Augustus was quite perplexed when the Queen's attendants left, and she directed him to a divan in her studio and instructed him to disrobe. He complied, as he was concerned by the likelihood of being arrested should the Queen realize that he was in fact an imposter. So, Augustus disrobed and posed for hours. Eventually the Queen momentarily excused herself. When she left, however, she locked the studio door behind her. Finding no other way out, Augustus escaped through the window, sans clothing. We laughed about that for days." Kingsley began to laugh and the children joined him.

With their meal completed and the recounting of Hollingsworth's encounter with the Queen fresh on their minds, the three made preparation to once again rescue Augustus. Kingsley had Livi procure appropriate currency, feeling certain that a bribe would be required. Jack converted the virtual room back into the library and gathered up his period clothing. Kingsley looked on disapprovingly. "Master Jack, I believe it to be wise if you would stay here this time. I fear that you may be wanted, and could very well compound the problem by also being detained. Mistress Olivia, I do need you to accompany me, however. As a man of color, my ability to travel unobstructed is limited. I shall have to pose as your servant."

Livi was aghast. "Mr. Kingsley, I will not let you pretend to be my servant. You are my friend!"

Once again Kingsley flashed his kindly smile. "And for that, Mistress Olivia, I am grateful. However, it is the only way to procure Lord Hollingsworth's release. You will have to play the part."

Though not happy about her role, Livi acquiesced. Jack in turn tried to convince Kingsley to let him go back with him as it was, after all, his fault that "Lord Hollingsworth is in this mess!" But Kingsley had a more important job for Jack.

"Take this, Jack." Kingsley produced the ornate key to the grandfather clock and presented it to Jack. "You take care of it. You are now the 'Time Keeper.' It is your duty to keep the clock wound and the portal set. Shortly after I leave you will have to wind the clock."

Kingsley walked Jack to the scale model of the clock that served as the time travel- setting device. "Remember to set all of the elements to zero so you can go to the present. After you wind the clock, turn the settings back to the current position to open the portal so that Lord Hollingsworth, Mistress Olivia and I may return."

Jack was flabbergasted. "You want me to do this while you're gone?"

Kingsley smiled. "No, Master Jack. Augustus and I want you to do this from this time forward. This is why you found us. You are now the Time Keeper. You and Mistress Livi are now time travelers. That has been our plan all along. Once I bring Augustus back, we will travel no more. You and Mistress Livi will carry on."

Now both Jack and Livi were astounded. Livi said, "You trust us to do that?"

Kingsley had no doubt, and he knew Hollingsworth felt the same. "Of course we do, Mistress Olivia. You two are the ones who solved the mystery of the clock. It can be no one other than you. It is your destiny." Livi smiled knowingly as Jack carefully ran his fingers over the key. They too knew it was their destiny.

Kingsley broke the silence. "So, let us make final preparations to rescue Lord Hollingsworth once again, so you two can embark upon adventures of your own."

At that moment Livi recalled the visitor to her parents this morning. Or was it yesterday? She had lost all concept of time. In any event, she knew that soon the manor would be sold and all of this would mean nothing. When Lord Hollingsworth returned, she would tell them everything. There was no use in worrying everyone about it now. In any event, she hoped Lord Hollingsworth might have a solution.

It was also at that moment that John Stearne realized he had stumbled upon something more complex than he could ever understand. Talk of time travel was surely due to the workings of the devil. But he knew Matthew

Hopkins would understand. He also knew that he would be well rewarded for his discovery. Stearne turned away from the glass of the virtual grandfather clock, through which he had been watching and listening to the time travelers, and walked back into his own time and to Matthew Hopkins.

# CHAPTER 12

# The Witch and The Familiar

As a part of the recompense for his services to rid
Colchester of its witches, Hopkins was provided
a suite in Colchester Castle. His suite was on the first
floor, which was above the ground floor where Augustus
Hollingsworth heretofore had been detained. The first
floor was accessible from spiral staircases situated in
the southeast and southwest buttresses of the keep.
Additionally, a staircase outside the west wall of the keep
provided access to the first floor through a large converted doorway, which Hopkins had reconstructed so as
to allow access to his suite without having to traverse the
ground-floor jail. The Great Hall of the keep predomi-
nantly occupied the first floor. In earlier days the hall
had functioned as a throne room for the King, and subsequently as an elegant ballroom. Hopkins had converted

the hall to a courtroom, over which he presided from an ostentatious dais. In addition to the courtroom, here too were housed his many assistants, also supplied by the village of Colchester. John Stearne maintained a desk there as well, though it rarely housed person or paper. The fact of the matter was that John Stearne was illiterate. His talents lay elsewhere.

The hall, unlike the ground floor, housed two large fireplaces, and therefore was not in need of hay to provide insulation and bedding. In fact, the hall was kept impeccably clean, revealing a stonework floor that dated to the reign of William the Conqueror. Behind the dais was a stone bulkhead that segregated a fourth of the area of the first floor from the hall. Behind this wall were Hopkins' private quarters. His suite housed a large study, a bedchamber and his personal privy. The study and bedchamber had a small fireplace each. The privy was in the northeast buttress of the keep, as were the privies of the ground floor and second floor. These latrines consisted of a stone ledge with a hole cut into it. They communicated with stone chutes that were built into the castle wall, and emptied from the outer wall at their respective levels over a narrow moat around the keep that in turn flowed into the River Colne. The nine square-foot segment of the stone ledge that contained the hole could be lifted to allow for cleaning of the privy. However, the chute was not accessible and as there was no running water, it could only be flushed by the occasional pouring in of water. The result was that the privies, indeed the entire northeast buttress of the keep, retained a remarkably foul stench that in summertime permeated the castle. But for the time, this was the closest thing to indoor plumbing, and it did negate the need for a cold winter trek to an outhouse.

It was in the study of Hopkins' suite that John Stearne revealed his discovery. Initially, Hopkins could not believe his ears. He listened intently, staring at Stearne for untold minutes, dismayed at what he heard. During that time Stearne came to regret that he had recounted his tale. Instead of being met with an enthusiastic reward, he came to fear that he might be imprisoned or sent to an asylum, as Hopkins' silent, piercing stare continued.

But then the silence was broken. The glaze over Hopkins' eyes softened and a slight smirk appeared on his lips. "Tell me again, Mr. Stearne. Leave out no details."

So, John Stearne did tell him again. "You see, Master, I was in pursuit of the boy. He ran directly to the house of Hollingsworth."

Hopkins interrupted, "Did you see Lord Hollingsworth or any of his family? Did the boy go to him for aid?"

Stearne continued, "No, Master. He did not go up to the house. He passed in front of it, jumped the wall and went around the west side." Stearne stopped, waiting for additional questions.

Hopkins noticed his hesitation and with all the patience he could muster, bade him go on: "Continue, Mr. Stearne."

"Very good, Master. I lost sight of the boy for a moment. When I rounded the corner, I saw him leap into the air, where he was engulfed in a blue cloud and disappeared."

Hopkins registered a thought. "Did the boy change form, Mr. Stearne? Did he perhaps become an animal such as a cat or a dog as he entered the cloud?"

John Stearne was not a very bright man. But he had come to know that there were times when Hopkins would ask a question with the intent of guiding the answer. Stearne felt that this was one of those times and carefully forged his response. "Now that you mention it, Master, I do believe that I saw a tail as the boy entered the cloud."

Stearne had presumed correctly, as Hopkins was jubilant at his reply. "Ah ha! There you have it, Mr. Stearne. The boy is the familiar of a witch! And the witch, Mr. Stearne, is at this moment jailed below us! You shall testify to your witness of this familiar, Mr. Stearne, but you shall tell no one of the time travel apparatus. Do you understand?"

Stearne understood completely. "I do, Master."

Hopkins once again interrupted Stearne's recounting and bellowed for his Sergeant at Arms, his personal bodyguard in reality, whom he also extorted from the villagers of Colchester. "Mr. Cook!"

Hollister Cook emerged from his station in the Great Hall. "Yes, Witchfinder General?"

Hopkins addressed Cook with a sardonic grin. "Mr. Cook, remand the prisoner that attacked me this morning to the tower. I believe him to be a witch. Who does he claim to be? I want to know everything about him."

Cook bowed in assent. "Yes, Witchfinder General. Right away, my Lord." Cook then took his leave to carry out the task.

Hopkins and Stearne both knew that the tale of the boy being a familiar was a ruse. This followed a pattern of deceit that the two had well rehearsed and mastered. Both knew that they would be rewarded. Hopkins seemed now much more relaxed. He took a seat and offered a seat to Stearne. "Now, Mr. Stearne, continue your story, please. I don't need to hear about Augustus Hollingsworth and his Queen again. Tell me again about the settings for the time travel device."

Hollister Cook did not care for the position to which he was commandeered. He had been the Sergeant at Arms for the village assembly. That position he had held for some time, and cherished. He did not like Matthew Hopkins and was wise enough to know the man to be a fraud. But like the others, he was hopeful that Hopkins would go about his way when he tired of Colchester. Cook saw what happened to those who tried to confront Hopkins and he wanted no part of that. He did have a family to think of, after all.

Nonetheless, Cook did keep apprised of the activities of one John Gaule. Gaule was a Puritan minister from nearby Huntingdonshire, where Hopkins planned to visit after completing his work in Colchester. John Gaule was quite verbose in his criticism of Hopkins, and in fact had published a book just a few months before entitled Cases of Conscience Touching Witches and Witchcraft, which was rumored to have a sound condemnation of Hopkins and his work. No one, at least to Cook's knowledge, had seen a copy of that publication. Still, tidbits of information poured into Colchester regarding Gaule's continued crusade against Hopkins. Cook hoped that Gaule's influence would soon penetrate Colchester and its populace would see to it that Hopkins' atrocities were halted. But for the time being, Cook was remanded to his duties. With a small contingent of castle guards he approached Augustus Hollingsworth.

"Sir, what is your name and from whence do you hail?" Cook was very gracious, as he deduced Hollingsworth to be of an elevated caste.

Augustus was relieved to see that one of the guards was unlocking the cell. "Ah! It is about time. Where is Kingsley? Is he out front? That man is an interminable procrastinator. I do believe I shall have to have a serious talk with him. So, which way out, my good man, I've had an elegant sufficiency of these accommodations."

As Hollingsworth made to exit, he was halted by one of the guards. With genuine regret, Cook informed Hollingsworth of his mission. "I am sorry sir, but there is no one here on your behalf. I'm afraid you are being moved to the tower. Now, will you please tell me your full name and place of residence?"

Hollingsworth was taken aback. "I'm being moved to the tower. What, pray tell, is the tower? And where is Mr. Kingsley?"

Cook felt his stomach turn. "The tower, sir, is where witches are imprisoned. The Witchfinder General has instructed that you be remanded to the tower. He suspects you a witch, sir."

Hollingsworth was now simply appalled. "I a witch? Why, that is preposterous! There is no such thing as a witch! Now, I should like to be released. Whatever the fine, I will pay it as soon as my associate, that is my man-servant, arrives. Now if you will kindly escort me out, I would be most grateful."

Cook had seen such innocent denial before. He knew that the man before him spoke the truth. He knew also that to Matthew Hopkins, the truth was irrelevant. Cook did not have the heart to tell this man what lay in wait for him. He felt another wave of nausea, this time knowing it was because of his own lack of courage to stand up to the Witchfinder General. He wished that John Gaule's movement had arrived in earnest. "I am sorry, sir, but I can only escort you to the tower. What is the name of your servant? I will apprise him of your circumstances."

Hollingsworth came to the realization that he was not to be released. He did not want to ponder upon what being accused as a witch really meant in this day and age. He could only hope for the prompt arrival of Kingsley. "Kingsley is his name. He will be along forthwith. I suspect he will be accompanying my niece and nephew. Kingsley will know what to do."

Cook, as though granting the last request of a condemned man, assured Hollingsworth that he would be on the lookout for Kingsley and his relatives. As they made their way toward the back of the keep, Cook once again addressed Hollingsworth: "Now sir, if you please, your name and your home dwelling."

Hollingsworth hesitated a moment, knowing that he could not use his real information. He spoke the first thing that came to mind. "Charles Dickens is my name. I reside in London, if you please."

Cook was satisfied. "Very good, Mr. Dickens. Please follow the guards."

Hollingsworth stepped out of his infested cell, leaving the drunks, goats and fleas to fend for themselves, and followed the lead guard. Cook walked beside him and two additional guards trailed behind. They walked to the back of the castle keep where they rounded a stone wall. Immediately, Hollingsworth was accosted by a renewed stench of excrement, which he surmised came from the guards' privy. It did not take much deductive reasoning to come to that conclusion, as when he rounded the wall his direct line of vision revealed a man in guard uniform, sitting upon a stone slab with his trousers bunched about his ankles. His face wore an expression of extreme concentration and his throat issued intermittent determined grunts. Hollingsworth was then led to the northwest end of the castle, where the lead guard had procured a large iron key from its niche upon the wall and was manipulating it into a keyhole housed within a very large, wood plank-constructed door. The heavy door swung open to reveal yet another stone spiral staircase, which the lead guard began to climb. Cook indicated for Hollingsworth to follow, then fell in line himself with the two other guards.

The path was poorly illuminated, receiving light only from the occasional slits built into the wall of the buttress that housed the staircase. The stone steps were slippery with dampness as well as a slimy substance that Hollingsworth deduced to be mold. The smell was reminiscent of a musty closet that had been closed off for years. The climb to the tower seemed unusually long. In fact it was, as the stairway ascended directly from the ground floor to the second floor without access to the first floor. In fact, this stairway provided the only entrance to the second floor, which served as the tower prison for suspected witches. At the pinnacle of the climb was yet another heavy wooden door. The lead guard once again placed the key into the keyhole and swung the door open. The guard stepped aside to allow Hollingsworth, Cook and the other two guards to gain entrance to the tower. He then entered, closed the door behind him and locked it.

As Hollingsworth entered the tower he noted that it was better illuminated than the stairway, but not by much. The windows cut into the original structure of the castle were filled with stone, which allowed only three vertical strips of approximately two inches through which sunlight could penetrate. All along the walls were sconces, which at present were not lit. He also noted two fireplaces, but quickly surmised that no fires had been contained within them for some time. The tower prison was designed for utility, not comfort. An iron cage had been erected to occupy one quarter of the tower. Within the cage were iron grate dividers, presumably to keep the prisoners segregated. There were small desks scattered about the room, as well as tables, benches, racks, chains and other devices that Hollingsworth surmised were for the sole intent of torture. At the northeast buttress was a quite exposed and easily identified privy. Hollingsworth wondered if he would be granted its use, as it had been some time since he relieved himself. He became painfully aware that he would not, as he was immediately ushered into the cell and the gate was closed and locked behind him.

One of the guards who had been following behind walked to the far end of the tower and sat himself upon a small stool. Hollingsworth surmised that he would be his sole companion, as no one else was in the tower and none of the others made to settle in. In fact, the others made toward the stairwell. Cook lingered behind for just a moment. "I shall let your servant know what has befallen you, Mr. Dickens."

Hollingsworth, fearing he knew the answer, asked anyway: "What precisely has befallen me?"

Cook was candid. "You have been accused as a witch, sir. Hopkins will move quickly. Tonight you will be interrogated, and you will confess. Tomorrow you will be tried and found guilty, and you will be hanged. It is the same every time. Unless some miracle befalls, sir, you will be dead by this time tomorrow."

Hollingsworth could see sympathy in Cook's eyes. "You know that I am not a witch, Mr. Cook."

Cook looked him in the eye. "Yes, Mr. Dickens, I do know."

Hollingsworth spoke with confidence. "Find Kingsley, he will know what to do."

Cook nodded and turned, feeling sicker by the moment. He moved into the stairwell and the guard closed the door behind him. Hollingsworth heard the tumble of the lock followed by the sound of laughter. He looked to see the remaining guard chuckle as leaned his stool back on two legs against the wall and settled in for his nap. For the first time Hollingsworth felt the cold that emanated from the stone floor below him. For the first time, Augustus Hollingsworth was frightened.

# CHAPTER 13

# The Interrogation

Augustus Hollingsworth sat upon the cold stone floor of his cell, listening to the snoring of his companion guard from across the keep. He was on the floor as there was no furnishing upon which to take rest. Hollingsworth wasn't there long when he heard the tumble of the lock. He rose to his feet, hopeful that his dear friend had come for him. He was sorely disappointed when he saw Matthew Hopkins enter, followed by John Stearne. Hopkins walked toward Hollingsworth and stopped just outside of his cell. He stared at Hollingsworth in silence. Hollingsworth returned the glare. Stearne meanwhile roused the guard from his slumber by kicking the stool out from underneath him, causing the guard to fall to the hard floor with a thud as the stool rattled a trajectory away from him. "Get up, you swine! Be off with you. The Witchfinder General wishes to be alone with this devil!" The guard scrambled to his feet and raced down the stairway.

Neither Hopkins nor Hollingsworth took their eyes from one another. After a moment, without diverting his gaze, Hopkins addressed Stearne. "Mr. Stearne, if you would be so kind as to take your leave. I should like to visit with the prisoner."

Stearne genteelly acquiesced. "Yes, Master, as you wish." With a curt bow, Stearne exited to the stairway, closing the door behind him, leaving the key hanging upon its peg.

Hopkins located a nearby stool, pulled it up to the cell and sat upon it. "I regret that I cannot offer you a seat, sir." He flashed his cynical grin. "Now tell me, 'Mr. Dickens.' What should I know about you? Or should I say, Mr. Hollingsworth?"

Hollingsworth was caught completely off guard. The look in his eye gave Hopkins reassurance that he was on the right path. "Oh yes, Mr. Hollingsworth. I know who you are. And I know from whence you hail. What I don't know is from when you hail. Perhaps you can enlighten me?"

Hollingsworth remained silent, not in an attempt to be obstinate, though Hopkins certainly perceived it as such, but because he was dumbfounded. How in God's heaven could Hopkins have surmised his identity?

"Come now, Mr. Hollingsworth, let us not dally. You, if anyone, know that time is of the essence. I know of your time travel device. My assistant has seen it. He followed your familiar through it. Now, you can tell me what I want to know, or I can extract it from you with the assistance of Mr. Stearne's rather proficient skills. Either way, witch, you will tell me. It is your choice. I will know of this demonic device."

Hollingsworth decided that Hopkins knew too much to allow for plausible denials. He met him head-on. "Mr. Hopkins, you know full well that there are no such things as witches. I know your modus operandi; I know how you think. Every old woman with a wrinkled face, a furrowed brow, a hairy lip, a gobber tooth, a squint eye, a squeaking voice, or a scolding tongue...a dog or cat by her side, is not only suspected but pronounced a witch. And for what purpose is that, Mr. Hopkins? To garner a few pieces of silver? To inflate yourself with an artificial sense of power?"

Hopkins was fuming now. "So you think you know me, do you, Mr. Hollingsworth? Do you think that your insolence impresses me? Am I to surmise that your purpose is to inhibit the services I offer to the Crown? Perhaps, Mr. Hollingsworth, you are in league with Minister Gaule? I assure you, sir; John Gaule, though a thorn in my side, is no substantial obstacle to me. And you, sir, are even less so! I further assure you that my services garner more than a few pieces of silver and that my power is anything but artificial." Hopkins momentarily closed his eyes in an attempt to bring his temper under control. He knew that to lose control was to lose the advantage. He spoke again, now with composure: "Mr. Hollingsworth, perhaps I was not clear. You will give me the information I seek. Your time travel device should prove very useful to me. But, to be fair, I will tell you what I do know. That should make it easier for you to fill in the missing pieces of the puzzle. I know that you are Augustus Hollingsworth. I know that you are from the future. I know that the time travel device is in some manner associated with the home of your ancestors. I suspect that you are in league with the present-day Lord Hollingsworth to derail my mission."

A thrill of terror went through Hollingsworth's body. "Lord Hollingsworth has knowledge neither of me nor my activities. He is in no way involved!"

Hopkins saw that he had struck a nerve. "There, sir, we disagree. I believe him to be quite involved. I assure you that I will link him to your witchcraft and will procure that property."

Hollingsworth was incensed. "You are a fool, Hopkins. That house in this time is of no use to you. That is not where control over the time machine lies. Leave Lord Hollingsworth out of this!"

Hollingsworth knew immediately that he had made a mistake. Hopkins realized his small victory with an evil grin. "So perhaps the home in another time is key? Perhaps the home in the future is where your time travel device is controlled? Is that where Mr. Stearne traveled, Mr. Hollingsworth? Did he travel to the future?"

Hollingsworth remained silent. "I take it by your silence that I am correct. You see, Mr. Hollingsworth, this isn't so difficult, now is it?"

Hollingsworth realized that Hopkins had enough knowledge to be dangerous. He decided to try to reason with the man. "Mr. Hopkins, you have no idea what you are getting into. One cannot willy-nilly travel through time. The consequences can be disastrous. What do you think would happen if you killed the present-day Lord Hollingsworth?"

Hopkins knew he had Hollingsworth right where he wanted him—in the palm of his hand. "Why don't you tell me, Mr. Hollingsworth? What exactly would happen?"

Hollingsworth bowed his head in defeat. He couldn't believe he had been so easily manipulated. "You are correct in your presumption that I am from the future, Mr. Hopkins. If anything befalls the current Lord Hollingsworth, then my ancestors will never come into existence. Ergo, I will never come to be, nor will my time machine."

Hopkins nodded. "That is exactly what I surmised, Mr. Hollingsworth. You see, I am not the imbecile you think me to be. Now let me tell you what is going to happen. You are going to tell me precisely how to operate the time travel device. I am going to take control of the house in the future and use the time machine to my pleasure. I will not be humiliated any longer by John Gaule! If you don't reveal the secrets of your time machine, then you will be responsible for any consequences that may come of my ill-informed travel. Tomorrow you will be convicted as a witch and you will be hanged. When I have completed my use of the machine, I will then have Lord

Hollingsworth convicted as a witch and hanged. The time machine will be no more, nor will the Hollingsworth clan. Surely that would not be such a blow to history, now would it, Mr. Hollingsworth? Now, why don't you tell me all I want to know? Otherwise, Lord Hollingsworth will hang with you tomorrow."

In his mind, Hollingsworth knew that he had no choice. He had to buy time until he could get in touch with Kingsley and the children. He decided to tell Hopkins what he wanted to know. But, he would not tell Hopkins everything he needed to know. Hollingsworth chose his words carefully. Hopkins wrote them down.

# CHAPTER 14

# A Moment of Despair

Sulking to some extent, Jack set the coordinates for Kingsley and Livi. They traveled to 1647 Colchester, leaving Jack behind. Kingsley had cautioned Jack to be certain that he set the time machine so that he and Livi would arrive in real time. Jack, somewhat dismayed, asked Kingsley why they didn't just go back in time before Hollingsworth was arrested and prevent the mishap. Kingsley explained to Jack two problems: First, that event was now history. To prevent it would be to alter history, which, as Jack well knew by now, was strictly against Augustus Hollingsworth's mandates regarding time travel. Secondly, in order to prevent the occurrence, the travelers would have to encounter themselves, which would disturb the time-space continuum. Kingsley did not understand the complete ramifications of such an encounter, but did recall on more than one occasion Augustus' warning that if a time traveler encountered himself during travel, the time portal could be irrevocably disrupted, resulting in the traveler being trapped in time with inherently devastating consequences. Livi offered a scientific theorem based on her knowledge of quantum physics to explain the phenomenon, but it was lost upon both Jack and Kingsley.

Kingsley and Livi stepped through the portal into the yard at the west side of the 1647 Hollingsworth Manor. They negotiated their way to Trinity Street and passed in front of the home en route to Colchester Castle. Kingsley presumed this to be where Augustus was being held. It was nearly five o'clock in the afternoon and the streets were sparsely populated, as this was the usual hour of the evening meal. The pair reached the castle at dusk and entered the ground floor of the keep through the main entrance. Livi was startled to see the floor covered with hay and livestock freely roaming the keep. She also noted the foul aroma as she passed by the prisoners in the cells to her left. Augustus was nowhere to be seen. Other people were milling about the castle and seemed to be settling in for the evening. She questioned Kingsley.

"Mr. Kingsley, what are all of these people doing here? Are they all prisoners?"

"No, Mistress Olivia. Only those in cells are the prisoners. These others are likely travelers who can't afford an inn, or indentured servants, or homeless. The castle serves as shelter for the night. They will all be ushered out in the morning."

As they approached the guards' station, Kingsley again spoke. "Mistress Olivia, you will have to speak to the guards. They will presume me to be your slave and I will not be permitted to speak. I shall stay back but will be close enough to hear." Livi looked at Kingsley with trepidation. She did not care for that scenario. "It will be all right, Mistress. This is the way of 1647 England."

As Livi approached the guard, Kingsley fell back. The guard noted her immediately, put on a most charming though rotted smile, and addressed her with a deep bow. "At your service, m'lady."

Livi glanced toward Kingsley, who returned an encouraging nod. "I am looking for my uncle. I was told that he was arrested this morning. Do you know where I might find him?"

The guard deduced that Livi would have recognized her uncle had he been in one of the cells she passed. In addition, by her appearance and the fact that she traveled with a slave, he presumed her to be of the upper class. He knew of only one prisoner brought in today who could possibly be a match for her. His happy demeanor faded a bit. "Is your uncle's name Dickens? Charles Dickens?"

Livi hesitated but a moment. "Yes. That is my uncle. Is he here?"

The guard stammered, "May I have your name please, m'lady?"

Livi felt it best to give her real name, knowing that it would have no connection in this place and time. "Olivia Hawthorne."

The guard bowed again. "Wait here if it pleases m'lady." He made his way toward the staircase and ascended. Livi turned questioningly to Kingsley. He surmised her inquiry and answered, "Perhaps they have moved him to a location more suitable to his standing. Knowing Augustus, he would not well tolerate these surroundings."

After a few moments, the guard returned. "If you please, m'lady, come with me. Mr. Cook, the Sergeant at Arms, would like to speak with you." The guard motioned Livi to the stairwell from which he had just emerged. Livi moved toward it and Kingsley made to follow. "Stay here, African," the guard said abruptly as he barred Kingsley's path. Livi rounded on the guard, incensed at his treatment of Kingsley. Before she spoke, however, Kingsley shot her a warning glance. "It is all right, Mistress. I shall wait for you here." Livi understood the message and held her tongue. She ascended the stairwell, followed by the guard.

Livi emerged into the great hall on the first floor of the castle keep, which was in sharp contrast to the level below. This is what she had always imagined a castle to look like. As twilight was falling, the sconces upon the walls were now illuminated. Livi scanned the massive hall in search of Augustus, but to no avail. She did see a small number of persons, some uniformed, others not, engaged in various activities. She saw the dais at the back of the keep, as well as a scattering of desks and worktables. Most were unoccupied, presumably the result of the late hour. Her eye did catch sight of a man who appeared to be sleeping. As she tried to focus upon that man's face, she was distracted by motion coming toward her. A smartly uniformed man approached. "Miss Hawthorne, I am Hollister Cook, Sergeant at Arms of Colchester Castle. I have been expecting you." He bowed his salutation. "Thank you, George, you are dismissed." The guard bowed to Cook, then to Livi. "M'Lady." He descended once again to the ground level.

Livi addressed Cook. "Mr. Cook, I am looking for my uncle. Is he here?"

Cook nodded. His expression was not happy. "If you please, Miss Hawthorne, come with me. I should like to speak to you about your uncle." Cook escorted Livi to an area near the dais where he kept his desk, opposite the place where Livi had noted the sleeping man. He offered her a seat. "Miss Hawthorne, your uncle is here. I'm afraid, however, that he has been remanded to the tower." Cook recognized that Livi had no understanding of the implications of his statement. "I would like to see him, Mr. Cook. I am prepared to pay any fine."

Cook was truly sorry for this young woman. "I can tell from your accent, Miss Hawthorne, that you are not from this region. Perhaps you are unaware of what has transpired here in Colchester over the past few months. Miss Hawthorne, the Witchfinder General has been in Colchester."

Livi was becoming alarmed. "I am aware of Matthew Hopkins and his witch hunts. What does that have to do with my uncle?"

Cook knew of no way to be gentle. "Miss Hawthorne, your uncle is imprisoned in the tower because he has been accused a witch."

Livi bolted up from her chair. "A witch? That's crazy! Take me to him!"

Cook calmly rose from his chair. "Miss Hawthorne, please sit down." For reasons she did not understand, Livi had trust in this man. She sat down.

Cook continued in hushed tones: "Miss Hawthorne, your uncle seems to believe that his manservant will be able to help him."

Livi lightened. "Yes, Mr. Kingsley. He is with me now. He's downstairs!"

Cook nodded. "Tell him this, Miss Hawthorne. Your uncle is in the tower above us. He will be interrogated tonight and he will be tried tomorrow. He will be convicted, Miss Hawthorne, and he will be hanged. There is not much time."

Livi was remembering some of the accounts Jack had related regarding the interrogation and trial of suspected witches. She began to feel ill. "Mr. Cook, you know that my uncle is not a witch. Will you help me?" Cook released a sigh, glanced behind Livi at the man asleep at the desk behind her, and leaned in closely. "Miss Hawthorne, I do not know what I can do."

At that moment, having left Hollingsworth, Hopkins emerged from the stairwell door. Upon his arrival, all activity ceased and those in the great hall rose from their seats and remained motionless. The bustle of chairs awakened the sleeping man, who then stood and moved toward Hopkins. Seeing that Hopkins was moving toward him, Cook rounded his desk to intercept him. He did not want Hopkins to know that Livi was associated with the prisoner in the tower.

Hopkins spoke as he neared Cook: "Mr. Cook, I want you to post two guards at the stairwell of the tower entrance. Keep a full complement in the keep and post a sentry to secure the perimeter of the castle. No one is to enter the castle until I direct otherwise. Is that quite clear?"

Cook, trying to position himself so that Livi wouldn't be noticed, said, "Yes, Witchfinder General. Quite clear."

Hopkins peered around Cook and looked Livi in the eye. When he spoke again, Cook feared that he was going to ask who the girl was. "And of course, Mr. Cook, you will have a guard posted in the tower."

Cook responded with relief, having felt he'd dodged a significant threat. "Of course, Witchfinder General."

Hopkins then addressed Stearne who, groggy from his nap, continued his approach toward Hopkins. "Come, Mr. Stearne. We have a busy night ahead." As the two turned toward the exit, Cook asked the question, "Witchfinder General, will you be interrogating the prisoner tonight?"

Hopkins turned and smiled. "There is no need, Mr. Cook. I have evidence enough. In the morning he shall swim the River Colne, be proved a witch and hanged."

Hopkins was downright giddy as he turned back toward the exit. Stearne followed behind, dejected. He would not be able to practice his skills tonight. Hopkins noted Stearne's disappointment. Certain that he couldn't be heard as they descended the stairway, Hopkins revealed his plan. "Come, Mr. Stearne, not so gloomy. Let us go sup, for at midnight, we travel to the future!" Stearne forgot to ask Hopkins about the girl with Cook.

Cook returned to his seat when Hopkins and Stearne disappeared from view. He addressed Livi, who he noted appeared dazed. Understandable in light of what she had just heard. "Your uncle seems to have a great deal of faith in the abilities of his servant Kingsley. I will help you, Miss Hawthorne. Meet me in one hour behind the stables. It will be dark then."

Livi, still dazed, nodded and rose from her chair. Cook summoned a guard. "Jacob, please escort Miss Hawthorne out."

The guard escorted Livi down the stairwell. She was indeed dazed, but not for the reason Cook presumed. Livi was trying to absorb the surrealistic fact that she recognized Hopkins and Stearne as the two men who had designs to buy Hollingsworth Manor. Understanding of that fact was eluding her.

The three travelers sat in the virtual library, and Jack listened intently as Livi and Kingsley related the facts of their recent visit to Colchester. They were operating in real time now, so they had to be off yet again to meet Cook behind the stables. This time, Jack would be going with them. There was no reason now for him to stay behind, as the worst had already happened. In any event, he felt responsible and was determined to help. He would not have stayed behind again anyway. Perhaps Kingsley had sensed that, because the suggestion was never made.

Livi spoke of Hopkins and Stearne being the men she saw speaking to her parents about buying the manor. None of the three could make sense of that. How could they have gotten to what would be their future? Kingsley suggested that there was not time to hash out a hypothesis. Time was of the essence. They had to find a way to rescue Hollingsworth. Then they could deal with Hopkins and Stearne and their journey to the present. Kingsley rustled up quick nourishment while Jack and Livi procured provisions. In no time at all, the three were ready to travel. Jack once again set the coordinates to arrive in real time. It would be ten minutes before midnight when they stepped out of the portal. Confident that all was ready, Kingsley went through first, followed by Livi. As Jack was about to go through, he suddenly remembered that he still had the key to the clock. With a sense of relief, he removed it from his pocket and hung it upon a peg adjacent to the scale model of the clock. How horrible it would be, he thought, if he had lost the key in 1647 Colchester. He then stepped through the portal and joined Livi and Kingsley.

The three made directly for the stables to meet Cook. Had they not been so focused upon their destination, they might have noticed the crouching figures in the brush next to the house. When the three travelers were out of sight, Hopkins and Stearne stood and walked toward the twine that marked the portal. Had they arrived at the manor but a few seconds sooner, they might well have passed the three travelers in the portal. As it was, they went unnoticed. Hopkins watched Stearne disappear into the blue mist. After a moment, he took a deep breath and followed.

Hollister Cook was a man of his word. He was waiting as Livi, Kingsley and Jack arrived at the designated meeting place. Though the night was cool, Cook was sweating.

Livi made the introductions. "Mr. Cook, this is Joshua Kingsley, the man of whom my uncle spoke." Cook acknowledged Kingsley with a nod. "This is my brother Jack. Jack Hawthorne." Cook extended his hand and Jack shook it. "Master Hawthorne. I wish the circumstances were more amiable."

Cook then turned to Kingsley. "Kingsley, your master has great confidence in you. I'm not sure, however, there is anything that can be done."

Kingsley replied, "Mr. Cook, how much time do we have? What is the sequence of events?"

Cook looked up at the moon before he responded. "There appears to be little likelihood of rain, so Hopkins will assemble the guards at daybreak. That will be about six o'clock. Stearne will come earlier, probably around five o'clock."

Jack interrupted. "Why will he come down early?"

Cook looked at him. "He will go down to the river and inspect the dunking boom before he subjects Mr. Dickens to the swim test. But..." Cook hesitated. Livi prompted him to continue. "But what, Mr. Cook?"

Cook looked at Livi, uncertain that he should go on. But he was resolved to help. Finally, he would help, he thought. "Stearne has something in the river. I'm not sure, but it seems to be a lift."

Kingsley became curious. "A lift, Mr. Cook? What do you mean?"

Cook explained, "I saw Stearne place a large stone into the river underneath the dunking boom. He then went behind the boom, where he was secluded by brush." Cook paused again.

"Please go on, Mr. Cook," Livi encouraged.

"He must operate a lift from behind the brush, because I saw the stone rise out of the water." Cook seemed almost embarrassed now. Realization dawned upon Jack. "That's how he does it! That's how they rise to the surface, isn't it, Mr. Cook?" Cook nodded.

Neither Livi nor Kingsley followed. "Wait, I don't understand," Livi said. "How does he do what?"

Jack looked to Cook, who in turn cast his eyes down. Jack offered the explanation. "Livi, do you remember me telling you about the dunking test? Sometimes it's called the swim test?"

Livi tried to recall. The truth was, however, she often tuned Jack out when he spoke. "It's some kind of test to determine if a person is really a witch, right?"

Jack was encouraged. "Exactly! The way it worked was that witches would rise to the surface because the water would reject them." Jack perceived that still neither Livi nor Kingsley understood. "Okay, look. Witches are supposedly servants of the devil, right? So they are rejected by water because water is used in Christian baptism. That's why witches are supposed to rise out of the water and innocent people sink! Get it?" He saw that they did not get it. "Mr. Cook, how are the prisoners bound and dunked into the river?"

"The prisoner is bound in a sitting position with his arms wrapped around his knees and his wrists tied to his ankles. A rope secured to the end of the boom is looped beneath the prisoner's arms as a sling. The boom is then swung over the river and the prisoner lowered into the water."

"Then what happens?" asked Livi.

"The prisoner sinks," said Cook. "But after about a minute, he will rise to the surface, near dead from drowning, coughing and sputtering. But rise nonetheless, only to be whisked to the gallows and hanged, having been proved a witch."

Jack looked expectantly at Livi and Kingsley. "Don't you get it? Look." Jack sat on the ground with his knees up and grabbed his ankles. "They're like this. It's like doing a 'cannon ball' off of a diving board. If you go into the water like this, you're going to sink." Jack saw that some clarity was dawning. "Hopkins has got some kind of lever-activated platform that Stearne raises to make it look like the prisoner is rising out of the water! He keeps them under just long enough so that they don't drown, otherwise they would be innocent! Then he hangs them because they have been proved a witch since they rose out of the water."

Jack stayed seated upon the ground while the realization of what he said took hold. After a moment, Livi addressed Cook: "Mr. Cook, you know about this. Why don't you just tell someone?"

Cook looked her in the eye. "Miss Hawthorne, you have no idea how badly I want to do just that. The fact is that if I were to do so I would be imprisoned. Or worse, my family would be. Those who have tried to stand up to Hopkins have met with death. He is very powerful. He has a deathly grip upon this village. A movement against Hopkins is on the rise, Miss Hawthorne. Sadly, it has not yet arrived in Colchester."

Kingsley stepped forward. "Mr. Cook, it appears then that we must procure the release of Mr. Dickens tonight. I assure you that after we do so, we will disappear and will never be heard from again."

Cook looked dubious. "I'm afraid that is impossible. The tower is on the third level, accessible only by one stairway. To get to that stairway, one has to pass through the ground floor of the castle. There are two guards posted at the entrance to the tower stairway, the door of which is locked. One would have to get past at least a half dozen other guards posted on the ground floor just to get to the entrance to the tower. There are no windows through which a man can pass into the tower. Even if there were, a guard is walking the perimeter of the castle and would be sure to spot any ladders, should you manage to procure one of adequate height. In short, there is no way for you to get Mr. Dickens out."

As Cook's words settled like a fog of despair, Jack rose to his feet. He began to pace, deep in concentration. Back and forth he went, occasionally stopping to kick the dust. Then with resolve, he approached the others. "We can't get him out, but I can get in."

# CHAPTER 15

# Passing in Time

Hopkins and Stearne, having emerged into the virtual library, found themselves to be alone. Though Stearne was of marginal intelligence, he did have a remarkable memory and thus had locked away all that he had heard regarding the operation of the time machine. Hopkins felt it to be not only his good fortune, but in fact his destiny to have so easily found the key that opened the door to the grandfather clock. Stearne set the coordinates to arrive in the present, their future, and when they entered the library of Hollingsworth Manor they once again found themselves alone. The house was deserted.

With minimal reconnaissance, Hopkins quickly deduced that the house was to be sold, and in that realization settled upon a plan. He intended to buy the house, control the time machine, and ultimately destroy it once it had served his purpose. After familiarizing themselves with the home and mastering the operation of the time machine, Hopkins and Stearne determined to travel back two days in time in an effort to approach the owners and buy the house. They did just that, entering the library through the clock in the early morning hours and stealing away quietly to the front door of the manor. Hopkins and Stearne emerged into the damp predawn air of Colchester and hid away until sunrise. It was not lost upon them that they would appear to be out of place, as their garments did not resemble those worn by the subjects of the glass-encased portraits that were on display about the house. With morning in full flourish, Hopkins and Stearne found themselves at the front door of Hollingsworth Manor. Hopkins nodded to Stearne, who in turn banged loudly upon that door.

Susan and Scott were just clearing away their breakfast dishes, having arisen early in preparation for their drive into London. The knock at the front door was so forceful that even from the breakfast room Susan jumped, nearly dropping the plates she was lifting from the table. She caught her breath, and the dishes, rested them safely back upon the table, and made her way toward the front door.

Susan stole a glance onto the gallery through the large windows that abutted the front door before she opened it. She saw what appeared to be a pilgrim. That is to say, a young man dressed as a pilgrim. This man wore a tunic and cloak with matching trousers. His boots were buckled, as was the tall, wide-brimmed hat upon his head. A second, older man was present, but not so elegantly dressed. He too appeared to be in costume, wearing a billowing shirt, worn pants and dusty boots. His head sported no hat, but rather a mat of entangled, long graying hair that appeared to Susan to be in need of shampoo. The older man's roughness was in direct contrast to the younger man's elegance. Susan, amused at what she presumed to be a promotional stunt for some upcoming festival, opened the door. "Good morning! Can I help you?" she asked, genuinely cheerful.

The younger man, removing his hat and bowing, replied, "Madam, I am Matthew Hopkins. This is my associate, Mr. Stearne. I should like to speak to the owner of this estate, if you please."

Recognizing the names but not quite able to place them, Susan smiled at the authentically spoken dialect and replied to the man in like character. "I am Susan Hawthorne, Mr. Hopkins. I own this house."

Hopkins was taken aback. How fanciful, a future in which women owned property. He flashed a charming smile. "I understand that you wish to relieve yourself of this home and its surrounding property. I should like to discuss terms, if you please."

Scott, having finished clearing the table, came upon the conversation. "Good morning." Hopkins bowed a salutation; Susan made introductions. "This is my husband, Scott Hawthorne. Scott, this is Mr. Hopkins and his associate Mr. Stearne. I believe they have come to inquire about buying the house. Is that so, Mr. Hopkins?"

"Indeed, Madam. That is precisely the purpose of my call."

Scott opened the door fully. "Please, gentlemen. Won't you come in?"

Susan and Scott escorted the men through the morning parlor and into the breakfast room. There, they invited the men to sit at the table and took seats themselves. Hopkins pulled up a chair and sat. Stearne backed against the wall and remained standing.

Scott spoke first. "May I ask who it is that you represent, and what is your real name?"

Hopkins appeared confused. "Sir, Hopkins is the only name I have and I represent myself."

It seemed to Scott the man was serious. "Oh, I'm sorry. I thought that with the costume and all that you were from one of the historical societies. And, of course Hopkins is quite an infamous name in Colchester."

Scott let the words fade in embarrassment. Susan now realized why the name had struck a chord with her. Both she and Scott were now somewhat uneasy. If these men were not in costume, then at a minimum they were eccentric. Worse, they might indeed be insane. Susan now regretted having let them into the house.

Scott continued, "Mr. Hopkins, what is it you are looking to do?"

Hopkins was becoming impatient. "As I have stated, sir, I wish to purchase this estate."

"What are your intentions for the house in the event that we were to sell it to you?" Scott asked, curious to see if his response might shed some light upon his sanity.

"Sir, it is the intention of your most humble servant to reside here," answered Hopkins.

"I'm afraid that this is all rather sudden," said Scott. "And really it would be best for you to speak with our attorney. He is the person that is dealing with the sale of the property." Scott pushed his chair back and stood, anxious to have these men out of the house. "I'll get you his card. Now, I will be happy to show you out."

Hopkins likewise pushed back his chair and stood, sensing a change in the demeanor of his hosts. "Mr. Hawthorne, time is of the imperative, I fear," he urged. "I am prepared to settle with sterling silver in the amount that you stipulate." Hopkins continued, "My associate and I have only the best intentions for this magnificent property. Shall we have an accord, sir?" he questioned insistently.

Hopkins stepped forward with his hand extended. Stearne stepped up close behind him. As he did so, Stearne saw in his line of sight a young woman, made eye contact with her and stared at her, sensing familiarity. He was momentarily startled when he recognized her to be the woman with whom Cook was speaking in the great hall just hours ago, no, centuries ago. Hopkins, noting his assistant's distraction, stepped forward and turned his head slightly; he too recognized the young woman. As he glared at Livi, he felt secure that the young woman had no recognition of him or Stearne. He pulled Stearne forward, moving out of the doorway and out of the young woman's line of sight.

Like Scott, Susan was now intent on having these two men out of the house, and did not notice their momentary distraction. "I'm sorry, but we were just headed out to an appointment and we really must be going. You'll really have to discuss your proposal with our attorney," she said.

Hopkins became more determined. "Madam, we shall return tomorrow with a case of sterling and the hope of finalizing a transaction. Perhaps your representative can join us then. I should like to execute this arrangement promptly. Shall we see you this time on the morrow?" persisted Hopkins.

"I'm afraid that we won't be available until tomorrow evening," Susan said, instantly regretting the disclosure of their return.

"Tomorrow evening, then. Now, we shall take our leave." After a moment's hesitation, Hopkins, followed by Stearne, made toward the front door and out. Susan and Scott trailed behind and secured the door in Hopkins' wake.

Susan turned to Scott after ensuring that the two men had indeed left the property. "Okay, that was weird."

"To say the least!" replied Scott. "I'll call Franklin from the car and make sure he's here when we get back. But you know what? I bet those guys don't come back. They were probably just playing some prank."

Susan gave a little laugh. "Or maybe they'll go back to the mental ward at the hospital."

Scott smiled. "But you know it would be kind of funny if they came back with a big chest of silver."

Susan rolled her eyes. "Yeah, real funny. I bet we can find someone with a little more traditional means to whom we can sell the house."

Hopkins was fuming. He was not accustomed to such nondeferential treatment. The sight of the girl flabbergasted Stearne. "Master, what about the girl? Surely she knows who we are." Hopkins was dismissive. He was more interested in how he was going to convince the Hawthornes to sell the property to him. "The girl did not recognize us, Mr. Stearne. I saw that in her eyes. We must go back to our time and..."

Stearne, anxious and confused, interrupted. "How could she not recognize us? She was peering right at us."

Hopkins stopped and turned to Stearne, sensing that he would be of no help until this issue was put to rest. "The girl did not recognize us because she has not yet seen us in our time."

Hopkins saw that Stearne could not comprehend the meaning of his words. But he knew that Stearne would be appeased by the fact that his master understood and was not concerned. As Hopkins pondered this, the notion struck him that Stearne suddenly looked much older. His hair appeared longer and grayer, his face more creased. Perhaps it was just the morning light. But when Hopkins looked at his own hands, they appeared spotted and thin.

They too appeared old. He thought it best not to mention this observation to Stearne. Instead, he continued upon his former train of thought.

"We shall go back to the house late tonight. The occupants are sure to be asleep. We must go back to our time and procure silver. Surely the Hawthornes will not refuse such a treasure. We will travel again at midnight."

Stearne was skeptical. "Master, they did not appear intent upon selling the house. What shall be done if they do not accept your offer?"

Hopkins flashed his sardonic grin. "Then, Mr. Stearne, you shall have to execute them. I will have the house and its time machine. But first, we must dispose of Hollingsworth."

Stearne returned the smile. He so hoped that the Hawthornes would refuse Hopkins' offer.

***

Having determined that he could indeed get to Augustus, Jack gathered the others to set forth his plan. "Livi, I need to have my climbing gear. Do you know where it is? You have to tell me if you do."

Livi answered earnestly, "Jack, I promise I don't know where that stuff is. I didn't take it."

Jack sensed that she was telling the truth. "Then I have to go back to when I last had it. To the day we moved into the house. I put it on my bed."

He and Livi, after some discussion and disagreement, determined the day and time that they moved their things into their respective rooms. That being settled, they called Cook over to join them, and Jack revealed the plan he had concocted to free Augustus. At the end of his discourse, Jack waited. He waited for objections, criticisms, suggestions, and amendments. None came.

Kingsley spoke first. "I should think it plausible. We shall all have to be in proper timing, but it is truly plausible." He looked to Cook, who posited, "If the boy can do it, then it will work." Livi reassured Cook, "Oh, he can do it. It's going to be pretty gross, but he can do it." She smiled at Jack. Jack returned the smile, feeling so proud to have the confidence of his sister. "Yeah, it'll be gross." They all started to laugh.

Cook took the other three in a roundabout manner to the river. There they inspected the boom used for the swim test and Hopkins' device that lifted the prisoners out of the water. They reconnoitered the banks of the river and staked out locations. Livi gathered reeds of varying length, curvature and diameter. She borrowed a knife from Cook and went to work. Feeling confident that the river portion of their plan was secure, they moved to the castle. The four hunkered down in the brush on the other side of the moat and waited for the sentry to appear. Once he did, they timed how long it took for him to clear the area.

Jack then surveyed the castle. He knew every inch of the castle in the twenty-first century, but wasn't sure it would correspond with the seventeenth-century version. It took only a moment before he spied what he intended to be his portal of entry. That accomplished, he turned to Cook for a description of the tower, as the third story of the castle did not exist in the twenty-first century. Cook described the floor plan of the structure. Jack felt that it was relatively simple and would not present problems. Of greatest concern was the fact that a guard would be posted in the tower with Hollingsworth. Cook feared that suspicions would be raised if he withdrew the guard. What Cook could do, however, would be to post the most inept guard of the corps in the tower. He would be sure to have some rye smuggled in to him, as he knew that to be his weakness. Cook was certain that Jack would be able to deal with him after a jar.

Jack made his way stealthily back to the manor. He would travel back alone. The others stayed behind. Livi continued to work on the reeds while Kingsley made repeated note of how often the sentry made it to this side of the castle and how long it took for him to disappear again from sight. Cook made off to procure a jar of rye for the tower guard and secure the other provisions. Jack was to meet them on the other side of the moat upon his return. As Jack neared the twine that Kingsley had stretched upon the ground, he checked to make sure he had the time coordinates Livi had written down, which he would need in order to procure his gear. Satisfied, he stepped through the portal.

As had been decided, Hopkins and Stearne returned to Hollingsworth Manor at midnight and, by way of Stearne's mastery of picking locks, made their way in through the rear entrance of the house. Quietly they advanced to the library and stood before the clock. Stearne opened the door, as he had the key that Jack had left behind. The two men entered the virtual library, and once again found it to be deserted. Stearne set the coordinates to return to their time and both in turn stepped through the portal, Hopkins followed a moment later by Stearne. As Stearne entered he felt the now familiar sensation of cool energy. He saw images whirring past him, giving him the perception that he was moving backward. Suddenly, he felt... What? What did he feel? Was it a bump, a wind burst? He wasn't sure. He had never felt anything like it before. He was sure, however, of the source of the disturbance. Standing in front of him, just as startled as he, was the boy who had escaped from him previously. Instinctively, he reached for the boy in an attempt to throttle his neck.

Jack was momentarily paralyzed when his perceived motion was abruptly halted by what felt like an electrical shock in the form of John Stearne. He quickly regained his composure when he felt Stearne's hands seemingly pass through his neck. Jack in that instant pondered how it was that Stearne's hands passed through him as he jumped back. No, he didn't jump, he willed himself to move back. Jack had never stopped to contemplate how it was that he and the others were able to travel through time until just this moment. Though he appeared to be as he always was, Jack now realized that he was, in fact, pure energy while in the portal.

Fortunately this realization was lost upon Stearne. As Stearne came at him again, Jack held him off with the force of his mind. It was as if he had built a force field around himself that Stearne could not penetrate. It was during one of Stearne's frustrated attempts to get at him that Jack noticed it. John Stearne had possession of the key to the clock, upon a chain hung around his neck. Jack knew that he must retrieve that key. He quickly deduced that he would not be able to grasp it. After all, if he was energy, so must be the key. So, Jack willed the key to himself. While holding off Stearne with his will, Jack pulled the key to himself with the power of his mind. The key began to rise and the chain lifted over Stearne's head. Stearne grabbed for the key but could not halt its egress, his hands passing through it. Jack's power was too strong and Stearne did not know how to manipulate his own energy field. Stearne let go a fierce scream as the key escaped from him into Jack's hand. Stearne made one last attempt to lunge at Jack, who adroitly spun and rolled himself past Stearne, who in turn landed with a thud on the hard ground in the year 1647.

Jack on the other hand fell backward into the antechamber of the clock, where he now lay gazing at the ceiling. He quickly jumped to his feet and hustled to the virtual library, where he closed off the time portal to prevent Stearne's re-entry. Then, he felt for his neck and head and assured himself that he was indeed solid. Jack sat down for a moment and contemplated the realization that Stearne, and presumably Hopkins, had not only discovered the time machine but also learned to manipulate it. He concluded that this was not a good thing, as he gripped the key tightly.

# The Plan

As Jack stood by the model clock that served as the coordinate control for the time machine, he realized that it was fortuitous that Stearne had not altered the coordinates, because had he done so, Jack and the others would have been trapped in the seventeenth century. Jack knew he must inform the others that Hopkins and Stearne had learned of the time machine. He was confident that Augustus would know what to do. First, however, he had to rescue Augustus, and this was no small undertaking. As Jack contemplated this, he set all the coordinates to zero. Before he could do anything, he had to go to the present and wind the clock. Jack entered the clock, fascinated by the mechanism as always, and pulled the chains that lifted the three tremendous weights. The portal would remain functional for another week. When Jack emerged from the clock back into the virtual library, he pulled the paper from his pocket upon which Livi had written the time coordinates for the day they moved into the manor. He hoped she was right. Jack set the coordinates to correspond, took a deep breath and stepped into the portal.

Now sporting the key on the chain about his neck, Jack removed it and placed it into the lock of the clock door. He slowly advanced it as he heard the now familiar whirr and tumbling of the electromagnetic mechanism. As quietly as possible he pushed the door open slightly when the lock released. He cautiously peered into the library, knowing he was there the day he and his family had moved in. He was painfully aware that he should not be seen by anyone, particularly himself, as he looked and listened for any activity.

Convinced that the coast was clear, Jack exited the clock and entered the library. He closed the clock door but did not lock it. He wanted to be sure that he could re-enter quickly. Jack stealthily traversed the library and made it to the door, to which he pressed his ear and listened. He heard muffled voices in the distance but could not make out the words. He did recognize that they were the voices of his mom and Livi. He knew that on this day, they were all unpacking and arranging. He remembered that he would be in the butler's pantry. Still, Jack was uncomfortable with his situation. He knew that if he were to be seen by anyone, all would be lost.

Jack cracked the library door and peeked around its edge. The entryway was clear, as were the two parlors. The door to the breakfast room was closed. Jack spied the stairwell. He knew that he would be most exposed on his way to that target as he eased through the doorway and tiptoed into the evening parlor. He was just about to cross into the entryway and up the stairs when he was paralyzed by his mother's voice, coming from the breakfast room.

"Jack, how's it going in there?" Susan asked.

Jack heard his own voice in reply, which he found to be very disconcerting: "Just about done."

His mother spoke again. "You guys getting hungry?"

"I am, actually," responded Scott.

It was the next exchange that launched Jack into action. "Baby, will you run and get the box of paper plates?" Susan asked Livi. "I'll make some sandwiches. We can finish this up tomorrow." "Sure Mom," said Livi. Jack heard someone jump to the ground, presumably Livi. He ran to the stairs and bounded up. He heard the breakfast room door open just as he rounded the last spiral. Jack prayed that Livi didn't see him, as he stood motionless at the stop of the stairs, listening for her to call or make her way up. He breathed a sigh of relief when he heard his mother once again speaking to Livi: "Thank you, baby. Now, do you want ham or turkey?" "I'll take turkey," answered Livi. "Jack, do you want ham or turkey?" Jack heard himself answer, "I'll have turkey." He cringed at the ensuing discourse. "Where did you come from?" Livi asked. "From there," he heard himself answer. "But you were just upstairs," she said. "What?" responded Jack. Just then he heard his dad declare, "I'll have ham." Livi, apparently distracted, did not pursue the question of Jack's whereabouts any further.

Jack decided to make haste, knowing he and his family would be occupied with eating for the next little while. He made his way to his room, avoiding all of the squeaky floorboards to which he had now become accustomed. Upon entering his room, he saw his travel bag on the floor and his climbing gear and magic kit resting upon his bed. He slung the backpack that contained his climbing gear over his shoulder and tucked the magic kit under his arm.

Jack made his way back to the top of the stairs and listened. He heard himself and his family engaged in casual conversation as they ate dinner. Jack snuck down the stairs and made his way back into the library. He gently closed the library door and headed for the clock. He entered the clock and listened one last time before he pulled the door closed. Satisfied that he had gone undetected, Jack closed the door, locked it and entered the virtual library. The whole experience had been quite surreal and, honestly, a bit disturbing.

Jack took a moment to inventory the contents of his climbing bag and magic kit before returning to 1647 Colchester. He determined that all he needed from his magic kit was the rope. He took it from the kit, placed it with his climbing gear and returned it all to his backpack. Satisfied that he had everything he would need to execute his plan for Augustus' rescue, Jack set the coordinates, entered the portal and returned to the past. He hoped Hopkins and Stearne would not attempt to access the portal.

As had been pre-arranged, Jack returned a mere thirty minutes after he had left the past and walked to the village stables, where he would meet the others. Jack arrived first. Within fifteen minutes Livi and Kingsley arrived. While they waited for Cook, Jack told them of his encounter with Stearne.

"Well then, that answers the question as to how Hopkins and Stearne came to be with your parents, Mistress Olivia," noted Kingsley. "But that means they can go back."

Jack became alarmed. "What can we do? What about mom and dad? What will they do to them?"

Kingsley felt Jack's concern. "Master Jack, Augustus will know what to do. We must first secure his release. Until then, Hopkins and Stearne will be able to traverse time as they please. We must act quickly and effectively."

Soon thereafter, Cook arrived. He reported that he had successfully supplied the inept guard posted in the tower with an ample supply of rye. "He should be effectively inebriated within the half hour." Kingsley reported that the sentry posted about the castle made the perimeter about every fifteen to twenty minutes. Jack felt confident that the time frame was adequate to accomplish his mission.

He set to work quickly with Livi. He needed to give her a crash course in belaying technique. Livi had seen Jack climb a rock wall, but she had never watched him climb an actual rock surface and didn't really know what it meant to be a belayer. She knew it had something to do with holding a rope so that the climber didn't fall to his death. That thought gave her no comfort. She now wished she had been a bit more interested in Jack's "stupid little hobby."

Jack pulled out two climbing harnesses, deftly put on his and then helped Livi into hers. He checked to see that all of the fasteners were secure and set to giving Livi her crash course in the art of belaying. He demonstrated how the rope was threaded through the ATC (air traffic controller) that would be attached to her harness. Jack showed her that just small angulations of the rope against the ATC would lock the rope into place. He showed Livi how to play out rope via a hand-over-hand technique so that she would never lose control of the line. Jack showed her how to brace herself and how to keep her hands from being caught between the rope and the ATC. The entire lesson took less than five minutes. Livi appeared unsure, but Jack told her that he was confident that she could do it. He hoped that he was right. It really didn't matter now. There was no time left.

The hour was one o'clock in the morning when the rescuers took up their position behind the brush across the moat. They waited for the sentry to make two passes. When he moved out of sight, Jack and Livi sprang into action. Jack looked like a Special Forces operator as he traversed the footbridge over the moat and sprinted toward the castle. Upon his feet he wore his rock-climbing shoes. He had a coil of rope looped over his head and tucked under his arm. He wore black cargo shorts, in one pocket of which was stuffed the magic rope. His climbing harness was in place and secured. Livi followed behind, encumbered only by her climbing harness. Even so, she found her movement to be restricted. Normally much faster than Jack, Livi found herself falling behind. She redoubled her efforts and determination. She would not be the cause if this rescue failed.

Jack made it to the plinth of the castle, followed in short order by Livi. They secreted into a shadowed recess of the castle wall where they would remain unseen from the sentry's vantage point as he made his rounds. Jack quickly retrieved the climbing rope from around his neck, and sat with his back to the wall as he deftly tied the first figure-eight knot and ran the tail through the front loop of his harness. He then traced the tail of the rope over the knot he had just tied, thus completing the figure-eight follow-through knot. Jack stood and went through his safety check, feeling disconcerted as he had never before climbed without an experienced partner to belay him and assist him with the check. He did not let on to Livi that he was worried. Jack tightened the knot, secured the tail and counted the loops, ensuring that he had six and therefore a slip-proof knot. He then re-checked his harness to be sure that no red was visible on his strap rings both at his waist and his legs, guaranteeing that the straps would remain secure. Jack then turned his attention to Livi. He had her stand up and checked the strap rings of her harness. It was important that she as the belayer be just as secure as he the climber. He looped the rope through the ATC, and with a carabiner attached it to the front loop of Livi's harness. Jack stepped back and looked up the wall that he was about to climb. Determining his route, he looked back to the ground for the best place for Livi to be positioned to belay him. He had her sit upon the ground with her feet braced against one of the many large stones embedded in the ground around the castle. Satisfied that Livi was well anchored, he reviewed with her again the technique of letting rope out, locking the rope in place, and pulling the rope back in. Jack saw that Livi was nervous, but he now knew that she had it down. He was ready to go.

Jack had a detailed knowledge of the stonework of the castle from his many prior visits, and had loaded his belt with medium-sized tapered chocks. Each chock consisted of a nut and a looped cable six inches long to which Jack connected a locking carabiner. He had latched the carabiners to loops on both sides of his harness, but did not lock them so as to be able to access them readily. Jack reflexively reached to his head to check the security of his helmet, and quickly remembered he wasn't wearing one. He had never climbed before without a helmet, but this was a different climb. Jack knew that he was not at risk for falling rock and he knew that the second leg of his journey would not be possible with a helmet.

Satisfied, Jack set to scale the outer wall of the castle. He looked towards the corners of the castle, making certain the sentry was not in sight. Jack then peered in the direction of the moat where he knew the others were waiting. He wondered if they could see him but presumed not, as he was well camouflaged. He set into motion with a nervous sensation in his gut. For a moment, he questioned whether or not he could actually pull this off. It took but an instant before he pushed that seed of doubt from his mind. It did not occur to him that just a few weeks ago, he would have been paralyzed by that doubt.

Jack mantled to the top of the plinth and stood upon its ledge. He removed the first chock from his harness and set it in the crack between two stones of the castle wall. He pulled it down to set it into place and snapped his rope into the loop of the carabiner and then locked it. Jack would set a chock every three feet, so that the greatest distance he would plummet in the event of a fall would be six feet before his descent was halted, hopefully, by Livi. Having set the first chock, Jack scanned the wall and his intended route of ascent. He planned for the last chock to be positioned just left of and above the access point to the second leg of his journey. In the darkness, Jack could not see that point. With his foot and handholds planned, Jack was ready to climb. He looked back at Livi. "On belay?" Livi smiled a nervous smile, tugged on her harness, positioned her hands upon the rope and took out its slack. With a nod she said, "Belay on." Jack smiled back. "Good luck!" he said, and he began his ascent.

Jack utilized climbing skills and techniques suitable to both face climbing and crack climbing, alternately smearing or edging with his feet while crimping or locking with his fingers. He scaled the wall expertly, moving rapidly yet deliberately. It had been some time since Jack had climbed real rock. He had climbed at the local indoor wall regularly, so his conditioning was good but his finger pads had lost their calluses. He was beginning to blister and bleed from small cuts and abrasions.

At the halfway point in his climb, Jack stopped to rest, allowing his weight to be supported by the last chock he placed as he massaged his fingers. Fortunately for him he did halt his climb. As he rested, he scanned the terrain below and saw the sentry rounding the castle in his periphery. Jack plastered himself against the wall, arms and legs outstretched, and froze, barely breathing. He dared not look to see where the sentry was, knowing that even the slightest movement might divert the guard's gaze upward. He hoped that Livi had seen the guard and was making herself invisible. Jack began counting off in his head, estimating that it would take the sentry a good sixty seconds to move out of sight. He determined to count to 120. After the count of sixty, Jack's hands, feet, arms and legs began to burn. He kept counting, sure that the guard would not take as long as he allotted to move off, but not wanting to risk early motion. The last thirty seconds of his count were agonizing. When he hit the 120-second mark, Jack turned his head just a bit to steal a glance down. Seeing nothing, he chanced a complete reconnoiter. The coast was clear and he gratefully relinquished his pose, bringing blood and relief back into his extremities. He looked down at Livi who gave a reassuring wave. Jack in turn gave the thumbs-up sign. Jack wondered if the others had witnessed the close call. He felt sure that they had as he continued his climb. He was grateful for the new moon, as there was no light to silhouette his form against the castle wall.

Jack set his last chock to the left and above the entryway to the next leg of his journey. He contemplated untying himself, thinking it would be less cumbersome for the next climb. But as he reached into the chute, Jack realized that the surface was quite slippery. It was not impossible that he could slip, fly out of the tunnel and be hurled into the early morning air toward the earth three stories below, with no hope of interrupting his fall. He opted to stay tied in as he squeezed himself into the chute through which the tower latrine emptied.

In the tower, the privy was situated in the northeast battlement of the castle, directly across from the secure stairwell leading from the ground floor to the prison. It was visible from the cell that Augustus Hollingsworth occupied. The latrine was built into a ledge over which a stone tablet rested. The tablet contained a small hole that fed into a chute cut into the stone wall of the castle. The orientation of the chute and the width of the outer castle wall resulted in the waste chute being roughly eight feet long at a declining forty-five degree angle. The chute opened to the outer castle wall, the waste being eliminated into the underlying moat. It was into this chute that Jack forayed. This was his path into the tower, and to Augustus Hollingsworth's freedom.

As a result of his detailed knowledge of Colchester Castle, Jack planned to ascend the chute, push the stone tablet aside and access the tower. He hoped the guard would indeed be drunk and unaware. Jack's intent was to inform Augustus of what was to happen just a few hours from now, and to instruct Augustus in the use of the magic rope, which would be instrumental in his escape. Most importantly, Jack was to verse Augustus in the details of the plan he had concocted and everyone's role in that plan.

The chute was tight but large enough for Jack to squeeze into. He knew that no one larger than he would fit, and that Augustus would not be able to access it. For a moment Jack thought how much better it would be just to bring Augustus back through the chute and down the wall of the castle. As quickly as the thought came, the realization dawned that even if Augustus could get into and slither down the chute, Jack would not be able to safely get him to the ground. In any event, Jack knew that he would be unable to spring Augustus from his cell. Hollister Cook had informed him that on the evening before a witch trial, no one save Hopkins and Stearne would have access to the tower or the cell that housed Hollingsworth. Once the guard was in place he would be locked in with the prisoner. He would not have a key to the cell. No one was allowed into the tower unless accompanied by Stearne or Hopkins. Even Cook himself would not be allowed into the secure stairwell. That was why it was so important that the guard be provided with ample rye before being posted. Jack determined that the plan he had devised was indeed his best hope.

As Jack pushed his head into the dark tunnel, he became painfully aware that cleaning the tower latrine was not a priority. The stench was unbearable and the residue of waste was thick upon the stone. Jack forced himself to reach through the muck to gain purchase on the stone, and pulled himself into the chute. He had to use all of his upper body strength to pull his lower torso through. He finally was able to push his knees against the sides of the chute to stabilize his position. Jack released his right hand and moved it higher to another slimy handhold. That being secure, he took another burning breath, held it and released his left hand. As he did so, he lost traction and slid back. He felt his lower body exit the chute before his fall was halted by a sudden tautness in the rope that caused him to be wedged against the top of the chute. His heart pounded, and despite the cold stale air he began to sweat. He was glad that he'd decided to remain tied in, and he was very glad that Livi had remained alert.

Jack regained his composure and purchased a left handhold. He pulled his body upward, bringing his feet into the chute. He found a foothold and began a more secure, albeit slow ascent. It was an arduous climb for Jack. In fact, it was the hardest climb in which he had ever engaged. He didn't think the climb would be rated highly on the decimal scale, but surely some credit would have to be granted, given the conditions of maneuvering a sewer.

It was as this thought passed through his mind that Jack looked upward and saw a flickering of light. He reached the top of the chute and looped his fingers over the edge of the hole of the stone tablet. He pulled himself up and was just able to fit his head through the hole. For the first time since entering the chute, Jack purchased a breath of relatively fresh air. He noted a single sconce bearing a lighted torch upon the wall, the source of the flickering light. Having been in complete darkness, the light was at first somewhat blinding. It took but a moment for his eyes to adjust and spy the image of Augustus Hollingsworth seated upon the floor of his cell, propped up in the corner asleep. He could see that his hands were bound with rope, just as Hollister Cook had said they would be. It was Hopkins' mandate that the prisoner be bound at night to increase his discomfort. That was the obligation of the night guard upon taking up his post. Jack was happy to see that the guard did indeed perform this duty prior to beginning his drinking. Otherwise, it would be hard to explain how it came to be that Augustus' hands were bound when morning dawned.

As Jack scanned the tower from his vantage point, he imagined how ridiculous he must appear as a disembodied head protruding from a toilet. He prayed that the guard would not have the opportunity to appreciate that absurdity, as Jack sought him out. From the privy, Jack could not see the guard but he heard the unmistakable guttural sound of snoring. Deducing that the rumble was not coming from Augustus, Jack was secure in the conclusion that the guard was indeed reaping the consequences of his overindulgence of alcohol. Jack lowered his head and set to dislodging the stone from over the chute. As Jack pushed up, he lost his footing and began sliding down the chute. He made himself as large as possible and came to a halt after about three feet of descent. It was the stone cutting into his arms and legs that provided the friction adequate to halt his exit into the dark morning air. Bloodied and bruised, Jack made his way back up. He again attempted to budge the stone tablet. This time he was well braced, and managed to lift the stone and slide it along the edge until he had enough space to crawl through.

Augustus Hollingsworth was dreaming of his childhood in school. He was admiring his teacher, upon whom he had a crush, as she wrote mathematic equations on the blackboard. Suddenly, the teacher's angelic countenance changed into the sardonic features of Matthew Hopkins, his fingers and nails, like talons, screeching against the blackboard. Hollingsworth was startled to consciousness by the torturous noise. He had just surmised that it was coming from the privy when the grating noise ceased. As he peered toward the latrine he saw a humanoid form emerge from its depths. He shook his head and rubbed his eyes with his bound hands, unsure if he was really awake. The form lifted itself out of the latrine and paused. In the shadows, Hollingsworth saw the silhouette of a small man untying a rope from his waist and securing it to a wooden peg that protruded from the wall of the privy. The silhouette slowly turned and moved toward Hollingsworth.

When the form entered the circle of light emanating from the sconce, Hollingsworth was shocked to see that the small man was in fact Jack, soiled, bloodied and bruised, with a finger positioned over his lips urging silence. Hollingsworth darted his gaze to the guard, who thankfully was totally oblivious to the happenings thanks to his inebriated stupor. When Augustus turned back, a foul-smelling but smiling Jack was upon him. "Hey," whispered Jack.

"Welcome, Master Jack," responded Hollingsworth in likewise hushed tones. "To what do I owe the honor of your visit? I'm afraid I cannot offer you much in the way of hospitalities, though I dare say you are in desperate need of a nice hot bath!"

Jack was relieved to see Hollingsworth's familiar smile. "Yeah, I'm pretty much a mess," he chuckled as he presented himself for inspection. "I've come to rescue you! It's the least I can do since I got you into this mess."

A small tear welled in Hollingsworth's eye. "As lovely as these accommodations are, and as gracious my host," Hollingsworth nodded in the direction of the drooling guard, "I am quite ready to depart. Tell me, young Jack, how do you propose to accomplish such a feat?"

Jack related to Hollingsworth the happenings of the day since Hollingsworth was taken into custody. He told of the events that were to take place at daybreak according to Hollister Cook. Jack described the swim test, with which Hollingsworth was familiar. Jack went on to explain the submerged platform and the mechanism that allowed the accused to be raised from the water and thus proved a witch, all witnessed by the locals. Hollingsworth found the discourse to be fascinating. He marveled at the ingenuity and genius of the Witchfinder General.

After a moment's reflection, Hollingsworth returned his attention to his unpleasant circumstance. "So Jack, what precisely do you have planned? You obviously cannot procure my release from this cell and I doubt that I could egress the castle in the manner you arrived."

Jack set to explaining quietly and with economy, as he knew dawn would be quickly upon them. "At daybreak Stearne and some of the castle guards will bring you to the river's edge. At the dunking boom your feet will be tied and you will be made to sit. The rope around your feet will be tied with twine to the rope binding your hands. Another rope will be slung under your arms and brought behind you, where it will be hooked onto the boom." Jack used his own body to indicate the orientation of the various ties. "You will be raised and the boom will be swung over the river. Mr. Cook says that Hopkins will then read the charge and you will be lowered into the water. Of course, you will sink."

Jack paused and Hollingsworth took the opportunity to comment. "Comforting. Sounds like a marvelous plan thus far."

Jack recognized the sarcasm. "It gets better," he continued. "Hopkins will allow you to stay submerged until you are nearly dead. He will then signal Stearne to raise the platform and lift you out of the water, and have you whisked away to the gallows to be hanged before you can recover from your near drowning." Jack smiled, satisfied that he related the information so succinctly.

Hollingsworth was not comforted. "Where, Master Jack, is the part of this plan that gets better?"

Jack recognized Hollingsworth's trepidation. "Oh, that last part isn't going to happen. When you're lowered into the water, you're going to escape!"

Hollingsworth gazed at Jack dumbfounded. He clearly needed more information. Jack pulled the magic rope from his pack and presented it for Hollingsworth's inspection. "This is how you're going to do it. This is a trick rope. It has a quick control release that can be activated by a flick of your wrist." The rope appeared as any other rope to Hollingsworth, until Jack gave it a slight twist and it fell apart into four pieces.

Jack smiled. "You see?" Hollingsworth was indeed impressed. Jack set to untying the rope that bound Hollingsworth's hands and replaced it with the trick rope. After a few attempts, Hollingsworth mastered the mechanism by protruding one wrist while at the same time slightly rotating the other, causing the rope to fall apart. Satisfied that Hollingsworth could manipulate the rope, Jack continued to explain his plan. Upon completion of Jack's discourse, Augustus broke his captivated silence. "Jack, I believe that is the most remarkable plan that could ever have been imagined. Well done!" Jack smiled in return. He almost blurted out that Hopkins and Stearne had learned to use the time machine, but realized this would not be the best time to let Hollingsworth know. There would be time for that later.

Believing that Hollingsworth had a good grasp of the plan, he took the rope that had been used for the binding and placed it into his pack. He checked the security of the trick rope and made his way back to the latrine. Jack took the end of the climbing rope from the peg and tied back into his harness. He then lowered himself into the latrine and slid the stone cover back into place. Jack once more poked his head through the hole, gave Hollingsworth a wink, and made his way down the tunnel to the castle wall.

Livi, seeing Jack's feet, pulled the rope tight. She was glad that Jack was finally coming down, having just hidden for the third time from the patrolling guard. Livi gave the rope three quick tugs, signaling to Jack that it was safe to come down. Jack began his descent after seeing that the uppermost chock was well secure. As Jack rappelled down, he gathered up all the chocks except for that top one. He wondered if anyone would ever discover it, knowing that ultimately it would come down in the future when the top story of the castle was demolished. Jack quickly made it to the plinth and from there jumped to the ground. He unclipped the ATC from Livi's harness and removed the loop of rope from the device. Jack then pulled the rope through the uppermost chock that he had left in place and watched it crumple to the ground. He quickly coiled the rope and secured it over his head. Livi informed Jack that the sentry had just rounded, so they were safe to escape. They quickly and quietly gathered their gear and darted into the night toward the river where Kingsley and Cook awaited.

# The Rescue

It seemed an eternity before Augustus heard the tumbling of the lock of the tower door. In truth, however, it had only been a couple of hours since Jack left. The hour was slightly before six, and dawn was only just breaking. Augustus had not slept since Jack left. He reviewed over and over again in his head the plan that Jack had devised. As the door swung open, Augustus experienced a sudden wave of nausea. He just as quickly pushed the nervousness from his mind and concentrated upon the plan for his escape.

Hopkins entered the tower first, followed by Stearne, Cook and a small contingent of guards. Hopkins motioned to Stearne to rouse the sleeping guard who had been posted in the tower. Stearne did so in his usual fashion by kicking the chair from underneath the guard, sending him to the cell floor in a heap of drunken blubber. Hopkins meanwhile addressed Augustus. "Up, witch, it is time for your conviction." Augustus rose, acting as though he had been sleeping. He was careful not to inadvertently dislodge the trick rope that bound his hands.

As one of the guards unlocked the cell and escorted Augustus out, he addressed Hopkins. "Shouldn't you at least pretend that there will be a trial?"

Hopkins merely gave his demonic grin and spoke to Cook. "Mr. Cook, escort the witch to the river."

"Yes, Witchfinder General." Cook intentionally averted his gaze from Augustus. Augustus in turn chanced a quick glance at Cook, whom he knew from Jack to be one of his rescuers. Hopkins then descended the tower staircase followed by Stearne. Once they were gone, Cook flashed a knowing gaze at Augustus and made his way down the stairway. Bracketed by two guards in front and three in back, Augustus followed with the last of the guards, who was rubbing his head with one hand and his backside with the other.

As Augustus and his escorts entered the dawn air, he was struck by the discomforting thought that the river was likely to be quite cold. He hoped that this would not adversely affect his rescue. As guards and prisoner neared the river, Augustus saw that a large crowd was gathered. Hopkins was waiting upon the platform built at the river's bank. Stearne was not in sight. Nor were any of Augustus' rescuers, save Hollister Cook, causing Augustus once again to fight back a wave of nausea as he stepped onto the platform. After receiving a nod from

Hopkins, Cook stepped toward the edge of the platform, unfurled a scroll and addressed the gathered villagers.

"Oh yea oh yea. Mr. Charles Dickens, you stand accused of witchcraft and demonic practices committed in this county of Essex, Colchester village. The evidence against you has been considered, and by virtue of his appointment by the Parliament of His Royal Majesty King Charles, the Witchfinder General shall preside over your interrogation and sentencing should you be found guilty of witchcraft."

With that, Augustus was forced to a sitting position on the platform and his ankles were tied together with a second rope. One of the guards swung the boom over Augustus. Another rope with a looped end dangled from the boom. This loop was positioned over Augustus so that it went under his knees and under his arms, forming a sling. The boom was raised and Augustus was uncomfortably hoisted into the air. Then the guard swung the boom around, thus suspending Augustus over the river. Hopkins proclaimed, "May the holy water of God repel your demon soul!" With that, the local parson began to recite the Lord's Prayer and Augustus was slowly lowered into the frigid water.

Livi was secreted on the riverbank just down from Kingsley, who from his vantage point behind the bush could see the platform. He gave the signal, upon which Livi entered the chilly water of the river, weighed down by two small bags of rocks suspended from her waist. Before her head submerged she place one of the long hollow reeds into her mouth. She had a second one that she would give to Augustus through which he could breathe. Livi skirted along the bank, hidden amongst the river grass along its edge. Every few feet she would steal a glance toward the platform, well camouflaged by the grass, and was in position by the time Augustus was fastened to the boom. Livi submerged, breathing through the reed, and made the short journey across the river floor to the underwater platform: Hopkins' deception. She had her feet securely on the hidden platform when Hollingsworth was lowered into the water. She hoped that Jack had prepared him well.

As Augustus was lowered into the river, he was surprised that the water was not as cold as he had anticipated. Perhaps he just didn't notice, as adrenalin was coursing through his veins. Augustus went to work quickly. As soon as his hands were underwater, he dislodged the trick rope binding his wrists. He immediately began working to untie his ankles. Just as his head was about to go under, the rope binding his legs came free and he took a long deep breath. As he became completely submerged, Augustus felt someone grab his arm. He knew it was Livi. She gave him the reed, which Augustus quickly thrust into his mouth and through which he forcefully blew out before taking his first breath of air. Deftly, Livi tied a bag of rocks similar to her ballast securely around Augustus' waist. Once fastened, she then tugged on the rope that was tied around her waist, signaling Kingsley to reel them in. Livi led the way underwater across the riverbed to the opposite bank, where Kingsley pulled them along.

Hopkins wanted to be sure that Augustus was near dead before he signaled Stearne to raise the platform. He waited a full sixty seconds, thinking the worst case would be that Hollingsworth would be dead. No matter really, that was the ultimate goal in any event. Hopkins gave the signal and Stearne began to raise the platform. As he did so Hopkins' eyes widened. Just beneath the surface of the water he could see the platform--yet the prisoner was gone. After a moment of frozen shock Hopkins bellowed to the guard, "Raise the boom!" The guard stood motionless, gazing at the water. "Now, you fool!" shouted Hopkins. The guard sprang to action and raised the boom. All that came up from the river was an empty loop of rope. The villagers emitted a collective gasp.

Livi and Augustus were well to the opposite side of the River Colne by the time Hopkins realized that his prisoner was missing. They were at that moment skirting the bank, concealed by the river grass and making their way slowly around the bend where Kingsley waited. Hopkins for his part sent the guards scurrying along his side of the river in an attempt to find Augustus. The guards had entered the river and were probing its bottom. After ten minutes of futile searching, no evidence of Augustus emerged. Hopkins screamed to the guards to find the witch as he started toward the castle with Stearne in his wake. "We must get to the time machine. That is where he is heading." Stearne presumed that

Hollingsworth was dead. He had so many questions but dared not ask. He followed along dutifully.

Livi and Augustus scurried up the bank of the river, out of sight of Hopkins and the frantic guards. Kingsley helped them out and wrapped them in warm blankets. Jack was waiting at the reins of a horse that was harnessed to a cart loaded with hay. Jack handed the reins over to Kingsley, then he and Augustus climbed into the back of the cart and covered themselves with hay. Livi covered her shivering body with a large woolen hooded cloak and climbed to her position next to Kingsley. Kingsley drove the horse hard until he reached the road, whereupon he made the turn, racing towards Hollingsworth Manor. He knew that he had a jump on Hopkins and Stearne, but not much of one. Kingsley whipped the horse frantically. Without relenting, Kingsley turned slightly toward the rear of the cart and addressed Augustus, shouting over the noise of the horse's hooves and the cart's wheels. "Augustus? Are you quite well?"

Augustus and Jack poked their heads from beneath the straw. Augustus was quite animated. "Oh my, Joshua! That is without doubt the most remarkable adventure yet. One I shall never forget and never want to experience again! I can't wait to get back to the library and hear how all of this progressed from your end!"

Kingsley glanced back as Jack averted his eyes and replied, "I'm afraid, Augustus, that the adventure has only just begun."

# CHAPTER 18

# The Dilemma

Augustus turned to Jack inquisitively. Jack registered the unspoken question and answered, "Hopkins discovered the time portal. He and Stearne have been to the future."

Augustus said not a word. He contemplated the meaning and ramifications of this pronouncement as Kingsley careened the cart onto the Hollingsworth estate and pulled in the reins. As the horse and cart came to a halt, Augustus instructed, "Quickly, to the portal."

Livi was first off and sprinted to and through the portal. Kingsley arrived next. He waited, watching Hollingsworth and Jack struggle to emerge from the hay cart. Augustus caught sight of him and exhorted, "Joshua, go!" He then jumped from the cart and landed awkwardly, twisting his ankle. Jack, who landed deftly upon his feet, helped Augustus up just as Hopkins and Stearne arrived on the site on winded horses. Jack helped

Augustus lumber his way toward the portal. Hopkins and Stearne advanced quickly.

Realizing that he was hobbled with his twisted ankle, Augustus pushed Jack toward the portal just as Hopkins seized him and knocked him to the ground. "Jack! Run!" he cried. Jack froze when he saw Stearne come upon Augustus and draw a knife. Without a moment's hesitation or an intentional thought, Jack ran headlong into Stearne. Stearne teetered backwards, stumbled and fell to the ground, striking his head upon a stone. He was knocked unconscious Jack then ran to Augustus, who was struggling to his feet as he attempted to pull away from Hopkins. Jack pulled Hopkins back as best he could, enabling Augustus to get to his feet. He could not, however, break the grip Hopkins had upon him. Fearing that Hopkins might get the upper hand and that Stearne would soon regain consciousness, Jack realized that he needed help. Seeing no other option, Jack released Hopkins, stepped back then bolted into the entangled pair, launching all three of them into the portal.

Kingsley and Livi never made it past the vestibule of the time machine. Just as he was about to re-enter the portal to return to 1647 Colchester, Kingsley was knocked back by a heap of humanity that subsequently fell upon him. As soon as Jack hit the ground he was on his feet, dashing to the control mechanism of the time portal. He had to close it before Stearne awakened and attempted to come through. Jack opened the door of the miniature clock and turned all of the dials to zero. That accomplished, he rushed back to the vestibule where Augustus, Kingsley and Livi had subdued Hopkins.

"I shut down the portal," Jack declared.

"Well done, Jack," said Augustus breathlessly. He then addressed Hopkins. "Well, Mr. Hopkins, you certainly present a dilemma."

Hopkins glared as he responded, "I shall have you and your family hanged, sir."

"Yes, I'm sure you would enjoy that," retorted Augustus. "However, I'm afraid that would greatly alter history with disastrous effect, so I shall not allow that, sir. Resignedly Augustus concluded, "No, Mr. Hopkins, I'm afraid that you will have to stay here with us." That pronouncement had the effect of a massive shock wave.

"What?" Livi exclaimed.

"Augustus, no," pleaded Kingsley.

With the concussive effect of Augustus' pronouncement, Kingsley and Livi both relaxed their grip upon Hopkins. In that instant of shock, Hopkins broke free and charged through the time portal. Kingsley regained his composure and made to pursue him. "Joshua, stop!" cried Augustus. Kingsley came to an abrupt halt, having understood. Jack did not. "What? We have to get him!"

Kingsley addressed Jack, "Master Jack, to what coordinates did you set the portal?"

Jack replied, "To all zeros."

"Precisely," said Kingsley. "That is your present, but our future. We cannot go there."

"Then Jack and I will go after him!" said Livi.

"It is of no use, Olivia," said Augustus. "Hopkins has sealed his fate. He will not long survive in the future." Augustus then turned to Kingsley. "Joshua, please lock the clock door and bring the key. We must discuss how we are to safeguard the Hawthorne family and Hollingsworth Manor until Hopkins is no longer a threat."

***

Matthew Hopkins moved deliberately from the library through the entryway and out the front door. As he made it to the street he looked back, expecting to see his captors in pursuit. They never came. Now two blocks away from Hollingsworth Manor, he began to relax. As he reached the center of town he started to feel strangely. He felt fatigued and his joints ached. He felt the eyes of the townspeople upon him and realized that he looked quite out of place. He determined to move quickly to the outskirts of town and hide away until he could devise a plan to take control of the time travel machine.

Just as he reached the edge of town he was startled by a deafening wail. He turned to the sound and saw a strange metal vehicle approaching, emitting a blinding flash of lights in the dusk. Two uniformed men emerged from the vehicle and approached him. Hopkins was too overwhelmed with fatigue to flee. The two police officers asked the old man who he was, where he was from, and what he was doing wandering the streets of Colchester. The answers Hopkins provided prompted the officers to take Matthew Hopkins to Colchester General Hospital rather than to the police station, deeming him to be a confused but harmless old man.

***

Having thoroughly discussed the events that transpired in 1647 Colchester, and weighing the threat that Hopkins might pose to the Hawthornes and Hollingsworth Manor, Augustus, Kingsley, Livi and Jack settled upon a conclusive plan. Livi entered the library from the clock first, followed in short order by Jack, who closed the clock door behind him and locked it. Just as he draped the key around his neck and tucked it into his shirt, Scott entered the library.

"There you two are! We have been looking for you everywhere. Do you know that the front door was wide open when we got home?"

Livi gave Jack a furtive glance, then addressed her dad.

"Yeah, about that..."

***

The Hawthorne family sat in the virtual library for hours listening with amazement, and at times incredulity, as Augustus explained his time travel machine and described his many adventures. Susan asked question after question about the technology. Scott queried about historical matters. After hours of conversation, Livi finally asked about Matthew Hopkins.

"He is a dilemma, Livi," Augustus affirmed. He turned his attention to Susan. "Mrs. Hawthorne, has any research been done on time and aging relative to the future? I have surmised that one traveling to the future would experience an acceleration of the aging process but, I have never tested that hypothesis."

Susan replied, "Yes, Lord Hollingsworth, there are quite detailed theories on the relativity of time. In 1905, Albert Einstein proposed his theory of special relativity and ten years later posited his theory of general relativity. At the same time, in the early twentieth century, Max Planck, Niels Bohr and others were also developing the study of matter and energy, which has become the discipline of quantum physics."

Augustus queried, "Would these theories or disciplines lend credence to my summation that one traveling to the future would age somewhat more rapidly?"

Susan looked Augustus deep in the eyes. "A person traveling to the future would not just age somewhat more rapidly, Lord Hollingsworth. The aging process would be exponential. For each foray into the future, the process would accelerate even more by at least a factor of ten."

Augustus nodded knowingly. "Just as I suspected, then. So Mrs. Hawthorne, is it safe to presume that Matthew Hopkins is now an old man?"

"He is likely a very old man," confirmed Susan.

Scott interjected, "So do you all think that he is still a threat?"

Augustus contemplated for a moment, then said, "I would be alert for him, or news of him, but I would not seek him out. To do so would raise questions that would best remain unasked. If these theories of time and relativity are accurate, I suspect that Matthew Hopkins will not long survive in the future."

The conversations about quantum physics, time relativity, technology and history went on for hours. Kingsley prepared lunch, dinner, breakfast and lunch again during the time. Livi and Jack went back and forth, retrieving and returning books, manuscripts and drawings from Augustus' secret study, which Susan and Augustus perused, debated and modified.

For weeks more, the Hawthornes and Augustus and Kingsley conversed and calculated. Jack and Livi received more and more training and instruction. At the conclusion, Susan and Augustus developed ways to improve the time travel machine. They fashioned a power pack that would wind the clock automatically, and engineered a remote device from which the portal could be opened and closed during time travel, thus safeguarding against unauthorized entry. Many other advancements were made, which led Susan to declare, "Your time travel will be much more efficient and safe now, Lord Hollingsworth."

Augustus replied, "I am very pleased, Mrs. Hawthorne. But these improvements have not been for me. Joshua and I will no longer be traveling through time."

# CHAPTER 19

# Going Home

"You see, Mrs. Hawthorne, Joshua and I have been waiting quite a long while for someone to unlock the secret of my grandfather clock. We knew that this someone would have to be imaginative, inquisitive, intelligent and adventurous. And when that someone presented himself, we would have found a special person indeed, the person for whom we have been waiting."

Susan looked at him inquisitively. "I'm afraid I don't understand, Lord Hollingsworth."

"Your son Jack, Mrs. Hawthorne, is that special someone," Augustus clarified. "With your permission, Jack will take my place as the Time Keeper and Joshua and I will make our final journey back home."

Jack perked up. "Me, Time Keeper? I don't know if I could do that! Look how badly I've already messed things up."

Augustus smiled. "Jack, you've heard Joshua's stories. Do you think all of my travels were without incident? You know how time travel works. You know the risks and how to avoid them. And, with the help of your mother, you have many more safeguards in place. You are destined to be the next Time Keeper."

Jack found some reason in that. "Will you help me? Will you travel with me until I learn everything?"

Augustus shook his head. "No, Jack. I will be going home. You are ready."

Jack made a decision. He decided to take that little seed of doubt and eject it from his mind. "Mom? Dad? Can I be the Time Keeper?"

Livi interjected, "I'll help him. I'll make sure he stays out of trouble."

All eyes were on Scott and Susan. Susan glanced furtively at Scott, who nodded assent.

"Jack, I think you will make a wonderful Time Keeper." She quickly added, "But you have to do well in school and you can only travel on the weekends."

Jack walked up to his mom and embraced her. Augustus smiled, a tear of joy sliding down his cheek. Joshua then approached Jack, and lifted the key to the clock that dangled from Jack's neck. "You are now the Time Keeper, Master Jack." Jack beamed as Livi gave him a hug.

Scott and Susan, hand in hand, marveled at the sight of their children. It was incomprehensible to them how much they had grown overnight. But then again, it wasn't really overnight for Jack and Livi.

Jack turned to Augustus. "What will you and Mr. Kingsley do?" he asked.

Augustus let out a soft sigh, as though the weight of the world had been lifted from his shoulders. "As I said, Joshua and I will go home, isn't that right, Joshua?" Kingsley gave his gentle smile. "Indeed it is, Augustus, indeed it is."

It was five days later that Augustus and Joshua decided all was in order; Jack and the Hawthornes were prepared; and they could finally go home. Augustus asked Jack and Livi to accompany them on this one last travel. Augustus had given Jack the coordinates so that they would arrive in the study of Hollingsworth Manor in 1896, precisely one minute after he and Kingsley had left those many years before. He then went into a virtual dressing room and put on the same nightclothes he'd worn when he first stepped into the time machine. Augustus emerged into the virtual library wearing an ankle-length nightshirt, a matching stocking cap and slippers.

Jack and Livi, who were waiting in attendance with Kingsley, stifled a giggle when they saw him. Joshua Kingsley, for his part, was wearing the same black morning coat, waistcoat and trousers that he'd had on that fateful day, the ensemble complete with pocket watch.

Augustus and Kingsley were upbeat. Jack and Livi were not as jovial, as they knew what was about to transpire, having been briefed by Augustus over the past few days. "Well Jack, is all in order? Are we ready to travel? Augustus asked.

"Yes, Lord Hollingsworth, everything is set," Jack replied.

"Then let us be on our way!" said Augustus.

"Children, after you," said Kingsley as he made a sweeping gesture toward the vestibule of the time portal. Jack and Livi stepped through.

The children having departed, Augustus slowly turned, taking in all the details of the virtual library. "This was quite a feat, was it not, Joshua?"

"Indeed it was, Augustus. Indeed it was," affirmed Kingsley.

Augustus approached Joshua Kingsley and placed both of his hands on his friend's shoulders. "Thank you, my friend." Kingsley replied with an embrace, as he shed a tear. After a moment, Kingsley released Augustus and stepped back as he took in his lifelong friend. "Tempus est?" he asked.

Augustus smiled and replied, "Tempus est."

Smiling fondly back, Kingsley said, "Then let us go, my dear friend."

"It will be a great adventure," said Augustus, grinning like a boy, "the best one yet." Kingsley took hold of Augustus' elbow and walked beside him through the portal.

Jack and Livi emerged in the Hollingsworth Manor library in the year 1896. They stepped to the side and awaited in silence the arrival of Augustus and Kingsley, not sure how they would react. After a few moments they saw a shimmering of light from within the grandfather clock. The door of the clock was pushed open and from it came Augustus and Kingsley. As soon as they crossed the threshold of the clock, they were transformed from the vibrancy of youth to their aged bodies of 1896.

With Kingsley supporting him, Augustus shuffled toward his favorite chair. Kingsley turned him so that he could sit and guided Augustus' arms around his neck. He grasped Augustus under his arms and lowered him to a sitting position. Kingsley then took a seat opposite Augustus, pulled his chair close to his friend, and took his hands in his own.

"Are we home, Joshua?" the frail old man asked of his one-time servant turned dearest friend.

"Yes, Augustus, we are home." Kingsley said.

"And the children. Where are the children?" questioned Augustus.

"Here we are, Lord Hollingsworth," said Livi.

Jack and Livi came over to Augustus and stood next to either arm of his chair, each resting a hand upon his shoulders. Augustus looked up at each of them in turn and smiled. He then directed his gaze toward Kingsley and said, "Yes, Joshua, we are finally home." With that, Lord Jonathan William Augustus Hollingsworth IV closed his eyes, and with great joy and peace went on to his final, greatest adventure.

# Epilogue

The Hawthornes neither saw nor heard from Matthew Hopkins again. No news was ever reported of him and the Hawthornes never sought him out. History is unclear as to what ultimately became of the Witchfinder General. Some accounts state that he was ultimately accused a witch and subjected to the same fate to which he had condemned over 230 innocent souls. Other accounts state that Hopkins died an old man, of tuberculosis. At Colchester General Hospital, two weeks after being brought there by police, a demented old man claiming to be the Witchfinder General of Essex passed away fitfully in his sleep.

Joshua Kingsley died two years after Augustus died. He stayed in the manor as caretaker until his death. The Hawthornes visited Kingsley often and continued to learn from his experience. Kingsley never time traveled again. He is buried next to Augustus in the Hollingsworth family plot.

The Hawthornes live in Hollingsworth Manor still today. Susan felt it to be her duty as heir to honor Lord Hollingsworth's wish to entrust the role of "Time Keeper" to Jack. The manor was never sold. The house, which is located on Trinity Street close to the library, is open during the day to the public (Tuesday through Saturday 10:00 a.m. to 1:00 p.m. and 2:00 p.m. to 5:00 p.m.; closed from November to March–the Hawthornes travel back to the States). It serves as Colchester's finest clock museum, celebrating not only Hollingsworth's beautiful timepieces, but also many other clocks, all of which were manufactured in Colchester throughout its long history. Not surprisingly, the most sought-after clock in the manor is the massive self-winding grandfather clock that towers above the bookshelves of the mahogany study.

Susan took a position as a member of the Physics Centre at the University of Essex in Colchester. She continues research in quantum physics and collaborates often with Gelman, who has since earned his PhD. Susan has designed and implemented many improvements to Hollingsworth's time machine. In fact, she has developed a process by which Hollingsworth's grandfather clock has become a perpetual clock, no longer in need of winding. All of her work related to the time machine is unpublished.

Livi has since graduated high school and attends the University of Essex, pursuing degrees in literature and mathematical sciences. She has received high accolades for her insightful papers on historical literary figures. Livi lives on campus, but visits home frequently. When she is not at home, she is sure to speak to Jack daily.

Jack now attends Colchester High School, where he is excelling academically. He no longer seems to have trouble finding time to study. His best subject? History. Jack is a starter on the cricket team (he has found his sport), class president, and is active in the drama club. His favorite hobbies, of course, are magic and rock climbing. He has scored many a date by impressing girls with his feats of illusion. Jack and Livi continue to time travel at every opportunity. Augustus would be proud.

And what of Scott? He, too, is active at the University of Essex, in the Centre for Local and Regional History. He has made great strides in expanding the historical databases of Essex and Suffolk. Scott has been prolific in the writing of historical novels. His most recently published book details the adventures of two children who time travel through a grandfather clock. Scott writes under a pseudonym.

# Author's Notes

The Clock is a fanciful tale of adventure in time travel. The Hawthornes of the story are fictional. Many of the other characters are drawn from actual historical figures. Though the author does reference real historical figures, and actual locations and structures, some liberties with the facts have been taken to enhance the story.

Colchester, UK

Colchester is the oldest recorded Roman town in Britain and one-time capital of Roman Britain. The town is located about 50 miles northeast of London and less than 30 miles from Stansted Airport. Colchester is rich in history, culture and diversity, and is home to many museums and nearby Essex University.

Hollingsworth Manor

Hollingsworth Manor is patterned after Tymperleys in Colchester. This timber-framed house was built in the fifteenth century, and was the home of scientist and physician to Elizabeth I, William Gilberd. The home in its current state is only part of Gilberd's original home. As a description of the original house is not available, in The Clock the author has patterned the large manor home based on similar homes of the era. Tymperleys at one time housed one of the largest collections of clocks in Great Britain, all of which were made in Colchester. In October 2011 Tymperleys Clock Museum closed its doors and most of the clocks went into storage. In May 2014 Tymperleys opened again as an event venue and tearoom. The Borough Council and Museum Services have allowed for a few clocks to be taken out of storage, and shown throughout the restaurant tearoom and first floor.

Colchester Castle

Colchester Castle, located on Ryegate Road in Castle Park, currently serves as a museum with exhibits that span 2,000 years of British history. The keep was built upon the ruins of the podium of the Roman Temple of Claudius, and was completed in 1100 A.D., some thirty years after construction began. The original floor plan was virtually the same as for the keep of the White Tower in London. The castle is the largest Norman keep in Europe, measuring 152 by 112 feet on a rectangular footprint. Colchester Castle in its current state is a two-story structure. In The Clock, when the adventurers travel back to the mid-1640s, the castle was much larger, encompassing four stories. Some authorities believe that the original structure consisted of four stories, and in the late 1600s a local businessman, John Wheeler, purchased the castle from the crown with the intent of demolishing the structure and harvesting the stone for building materials. After removing the top two stories, the venture proved unprofitable and the demolition ceased. Others, however, make note that the peaceful region of Colchester would not merit a tall structure; due to the lack of local stone, the castle likely only had two, possibly three stories, and Wheeler removed a portion of the upper structure. In 1720, Charles Grey, who would ultimately become a Member of Parliament from Colchester, purchased the castle and restored it to its original state, with Romanesque features added to the façade to reflect the castle's Roman connections.

Queen Victoria

Victoria was born in 1819. At the age of eighteen, in 1837, she ascended to the throne upon the death of her father Edward, Duke of Kent. As a young woman, Victoria was quite lively, far removed from the solemn, repressed widow of her later years. She had a passion and talent for drawing and painting, particularly nudes. In The Clock, Augustus' encounter with Queen Victoria occurs in 1843, the sixth year of her reign, when she would have been twenty-four years old, still quite interested in drawing, steam locomotives and journaling.

Charles Dickens

Charles Dickens is a young newspaper reporter in Colchester when Livi encounters him in 1835 in The Clock; he would have been twenty-three years old. By this time he had already been submitting sketches to various magazines under the pseudonym "Boz." Dickens drew from his own life as an impoverished child in his writing. Oliver Twist was published in installments beginning in 1836.

The Worshipful Company of Clockmakers
The Worshipful Company of Clockmakers was established by Royal Charter in 1631. This guild is the oldest horological institution in the world.

Samuel Downum
Samuel Downum began his clock-making apprenticeship with John Smorthwaite in 1737. Two years into the apprenticeship, Smorthwaite died and Downum's apprenticeship was transferred to Smorthwaite's former apprentice, Nathaniel Hedge. Downum, however, was not quite contemporary with Augustus. He would have been about ninety years old when Augustus was born. Downum died in 1769, forty-four years before Augustus' birth.

Matthew Hopkins
Matthew Hopkins claimed to have a special commission from Parliament as the Witchfinder General. He took advantage of the witch craze that erupted during the civil war in England. Hopkins used torture, which was against the law, as the tool to gain confessions. By the end of 1646, Hopkins abandoned his witch hunts,

largely because of a change in public opinion brought on by John Gaule (see below), and returned to his hometown of Manningtree. It is unclear what became of Hopkins. William Andrews, a writer on Essex folklore, wrote in Bygone Essex (1892) that while passing through Suffolk, Hopkins was himself accused of witchcraft and either drowned undergoing the "swim test" or was hanged shortly thereafter. However, John Stearne, his prime assistant (see below), wrote in his book A Confirmation and Discovery of Witchcraft (London 1648) that Hopkins died "peacefully after a long sickness of consumption" (tuberculosis). This is the most likely scenario.

John Stearne

In The Clock John Stearne is depicted as an uneducated and somewhat simple man. He was anything but. John Stearne was a landowner and family man. He met Matthew Hopkins, the self-proclaimed Witchfinder General, in Manningtree and was there appointed as his assistant. Stearne was ten years older than Hopkins and of the same fervent Puritan ideology. He was integral in procuring convictions of "witches" at Hopkins' trials. After Hopkins' death in 1647, Stearne continued witch hunting for about a year, but the witchcraft craze was dying out. In 1648, Stearne wrote A Confirmation and Discovery of Witchcraft as a defense against charges raised by John Gaule of hypocrisy and chicanery on the part of the witch hunters.

John Gaule

John Gaule, an old country parson, was the Vicar of Great Staughton in Huntingdonshire. He did not reside in Colchester but he did preach against Hopkins when learning of his planned trip to Great Staughton. Gaule gathered evidence of Hopkins' extreme methods and use of torture. He published his findings in Select Cases of Conscience Touching Witches and Witchcraft (London, 1646). Though Hopkins opted to avoid Great Staughton, Gaule's work was instrumental in turning the tide of public opinion against him.